CANDLES IN THE DARK

by

LOUISE BATES

To Dad, who makes the stories about "the old days" in Canton come alive

First Edition

ISBN: 978-0-9899551-5-7

Cover Design by Louise Bates Ayers

CHAPTER ONE

Anonymous Letters

A patchwork quilt of orange, red, gold, and brown covered the ground in preparation for its winter's nap. Pauline Gray couldn't help but scuffle her boots through the welter of leaves on the sidewalk as though she were a schoolgirl again instead of an independent woman of twenty-eight who had finished delivering her latest interest piece to the new post office. The "crunch-crunch" under her feet brought a smile of pure delight to her usually pensive face, as did the vault of piercingly blue sky above her head. A whiff of smoke from someone burning a leaf pile drifted past her nose, causing it to twitch in enjoyment.

Autumn was the finest time of year in northern New York state, there was no question about it. Even the economic troubles shaking the entire nation in 1933 couldn't spoil the charm of an October day in the foothills of the Adirondack mountains.

Pauline buried her hands in the pockets of her plaid wool skirt and paced on, mulling over the opening paragraph of her next novel. She wished she could set in here, in the village of Canton, but she doubted her readers would believe romance and adventure could be found in a small rural town. She herself doubted it. Canton was as placid and peaceful a place as she'd ever known, not a hotbed of excitement. She wouldn't have it any other way.

That aura of calm around the town was the main reason she had stayed here after graduating from St. Lawrence University and starting her column for the semi-local *Watertown Daily Times*. The town had accepted her as an eccentric spinster and over time began to boast of her as one of their intellectual lights. She kept her other writing career a tightly-bound secret.

Pauline would never dare show her face at the college again if her former professors and classmates discovered she wrote cheap adventure novels on the side.

She wasn't ashamed of them on her own account, or so she told herself. They gave enjoyment to hundreds of people and helped pay her share of the rent and grocery bill. It just wasn't—exactly—what people had expected of the brilliant, fiercely ambitious student when she had graduated from St. Lawrence near the top of her class six years ago. Rather than face their disappointment or scorn, she kept that part of her life private.

The air was so invigorating and the sun so pleasant on her crimson beret that Pauline abandoned her original plan to write for a few hours at the university library and turned her steps toward the park instead. She strolled down the path leading to the fountain in the park's center, dreamily thinking of nothing in particular. Her steps checked when she saw Ruby Ferris sitting on one of the benches bordering the path, her reddened eyes and nose showing signs of recent tears.

For a moment, Pauline considered turning back. She liked Ruby well enough, but she didn't want this glorious day spoiled by anyone's grief.

Then she set her lips and quickened her pace to reach Ruby sooner. Shame! Ruby had enough troubles to make anyone weep: a widow with a young son, her husband killed four years ago in an accident at the nearby grist mill. She never burdened her friends or neighbors with her troubles, quietly persevering and making ends meet. She worked as a cook in one of the local restaurants during the day while her son was in school and took in sewing to do at night.

For her to be seen distraught in public, something must be terribly wrong. Pauline could not be so selfish as to shy away from sharing, and perhaps thereby lightening, her load.

"Good afternoon, Ruby," Pauline said in her clear, cool voice, coming to a stop before the bench. Rather than look down upon the other woman, she sat beside her.

Ruby glanced up, eyes blinking rapidly, unable to meet Pauline's gaze. She had been a pretty woman a few years ago, with long, shining black hair and strong features inherited from her Iroquois grandmother. Sorrow and hard work had dulled the luster in her once-bright brown eyes and had engraved lines across her face. Pauline felt another pang of pity.

"Oh ... Pauline," Ruby said. She straightened her back and attempted a smile. "I'm so sorry, I didn't even see you. How are you today?"

She clearly did not want to talk about her troubles. Pauline's distaste for interfering or being interfered with struggled against her compassion, and lost.

"I am well, but you seem unhappy," she said, gentling her voice as she would for a skittish horse or unhappy child. "Is it anything I can help with?"

Ruby's lips trembled, but she shook her head. "I don't want to burden you."

"It isn't a burden if I ask for it," Pauline said, nudging Ruby's arm companionably with her elbow. "Truly, I don't mean to pry, but if you want someone to listen, my ears are at your service."

For a moment, it seemed Ruby would speak. Then, as a couple strolled arm-in-arm past them, with a small child darting around them shrieking with delight, she changed her mind.

"You are very kind, but I'll be fine. I'd best be off. Almost time to pick Jeremy up from school."

She rose to her feet and walked away swiftly, her shoes tap-tapping against the sidewalk in a staccato accompaniment to the nervous clenching and unclenching of her hands.

Pauline frowned after her retreating back, then stood up decisively. Perhaps she was meddling in an unwarranted fashion, but she didn't think so. Folks looked out for each other in small towns. Right now, Ruby needed a shoulder to lean on, even if it wasn't Pauline's.

Leaving the park to the young family, Pauline made her way toward the Town Hall. She mounted the smooth stone steps and slipped through the big front doors just as a wave of town councilors, reporters, and policemen left the building.

The massive stone Town Hall building held much more than records and civil servants. It also was home to the local branch of the *Watertown Daily Times*; a newsstand; a gift shop; and most relevant to Pauline's current needs, the village police.

She was in luck. Her quarry was behind the main rush of policemen finishing their shift, though already wearing a warm coat and wool scarf, hat in hand. Lieutenant James Richardson's warm blue eyes fell on her and crinkled as he smiled.

"Hello, Pauline!" he greeted her with a wave of his hat. "What brings you here?"

"Looking for you," she responded, the relative emptiness of the hallway allowing her to speak freely.

She and James were friends, nothing more, but seeking a man out could ruin a single woman's reputation. Not to mention it would earn James unending teasing from his colleagues.

His eyebrows went up. "Trouble? Or do you need my expert opinion on an article?"

She shook her head and motioned to the door. They stepped back out into the mellow October sunshine.

"Sarah vetted my most recent article," she said, naming the woman with whom she shared an apartment. "I'm here about Ruby."

James stopped. He spun around to look Pauline full in the face. "Ruby Ferris? What do you know about that business?"

Pauline stepped back. That was not the reaction she'd anticipated. "What business? I came to tell you she seemed troubled but wouldn't tell me why. I hoped you could sound her out and perhaps help her with whatever it was."

Everyone knew James and Ruby were seeing each other; the village confidently expected news of their engagement any day. It was a good thing all the way around, everyone agreed. James needed a wife to stop him breaking hearts, and Ruby and her young Jeremy needed a man.

Pauline hated that phrase: "needing a man," as though any man was needed regardless of character or personality, but she agreed that James and Ruby were well-suited to each other, and Jeremy would do well with a kind, honest father.

Now, under James' piercing stare, she flushed, wondering if he thought her too presumptuous. "I wouldn't normally interfere, but Ruby is usually so self-contained, and she seemed so miserable, and I couldn't walk away without doing something to help," she said, tripping over her words.

James' expression softened and he started walking again. "I'm not upset with you, Pauline. I'm thankful Ruby has such caring friends. Unlike some!" His mouth closed with a snap.

Exasperation stirred in Pauline's chest, replacing the uncertainty of but a moment before. "Then do you mind explaining yourself?"

He walked a few paces without saying anything, his hand creeping up to run his clean-shaven, square chin. Pauline was not a small woman, but she almost had to trot to keep up with his strides. Finally, he spoke.

"Maybe I'm betraying her confidence by telling you this, but I believe you can keep it to yourself. A few weeks ago, Ruby started getting letters. Anonymous letters."

"Oh my," said Pauline. That sounded ominous.

"They stated, in varying forms, that her husband's death was not an accident, but murder. They didn't accuse anyone in particular, but the writer 'thought you ought to know,' or so she said."

"How cruel!" Pauline cried. Hadn't Ruby enough to endure without having that sort of thing thrown at her? "No wonder she's so upset." A thought occurred to her. "You said 'she.' Do you know the writer?"

James shook his head and shrugged. "I'm assuming a woman because anonymous letters usually are," he said. He caught her ironic look. "It's a proven fact," he defended himself.

Pauline sighed. "I suppose so. Are you looking into it for her?"

"Unofficially. It's not a police matter, since the letter writer hasn't threatened her or done anything illegal. I've already checked fingerprints, handwriting, stamps, all that, but so far nothing has given me a clue into her identity. I don't mind telling you I'm about at my wits' end."

Pauline rubbed the bridge of her nose. "It seems so senseless," she said. "Why say something like that? They're not trying to get money out of her, she's a harmless creature so no one would want to injure her specifically ... James. You don't think it's true?"

"No!" he said. "Darn it, Pauline. This is the danger of anonymous letters, you see? They start people wondering, and muttering, and the next thing you know, accusations are flying and people get hurt. Don't even think it."

"Sorry," she apologized, but even his impassioned words couldn't stop her from wondering, mainly because she could imagine no other reason for someone to write something of the sort to poor Ruby.

"If it was true, this person would have come to the proper authorities," James said, sounding stuffy. "Anonymous letter writers are only in it for themselves. They get some sort of sick satisfaction out of causing pain to other people." He stopped and cast a glance at her, checking to see if he'd offended her sensibilities. Pauline's calm face reassured him. "My main concern is what this is doing to Ruby's nerves, and what happens if the letter-writer decides to move on to somebody else. If she— or he—isn't satisfied with one victim, we could have an epidemic on our hands. For all we know, it could already be happening. Anyone could be getting letters and be too ashamed to admit it."

"What can I do to help?" Pauline asked.

"You don't want to get involved in this," he protested, but weakly.

"Ruby is my friend, as are you," she said. "You already said the police can't take the case, and you don't know what else to do. You need help, and I am available." She smiled. "People expect me to do odd things anyway. You'd be amazed what a writer can get away with. Come now, James, give me a task or I shall start snooping around on my own, and who knows what sort of a mess I'll make of things then?"

"You don't play fair," he grumbled.

"That's because I'm not playing," she said, smiling sweetly.

He capitulated. "Talk to people. Chat, you know? Don't go asking any obvious questions, just get a feel for things. Oh, and here."

He dug a scrap of paper out of his pocket and handed it over. "This is a handwriting sample. See if you can match it to anyone. Ask them to write you out a recipe or something. But be careful, Pauline!"

"I will," Pauline said, glancing at the paper.

It read: *thot you shud no your husbant dint dye on axident.*

Pauline grimaced, feeling as though she had touched something slimy and decaying. She tucked the paper into her bag, resisting the urge to scrub her hand against her skirt. Briefly, she regretted getting involved in this at all. So ugly!

Uglier still to know about it and do nothing.

"I'll let you know once I've found something," she promised James.

He smiled wanly. "Once, not if, eh? I like your optimism."

It was spoken more bravely than Pauline felt, but she was determined to succeed, no matter how difficult the task. The sooner this letter-writer was found, the sooner Canton could return to its tranquil existence, the one that soothed her often-turbulent spirit so well.

For all that Pauline preferred an orderly, calm life, she found herself restless and anxious more often than not. It had been especially bad during high school, the normal emotional turmoil of adolescence made worse by inner storms that would sweep across her soul on a frequent basis, leaving her shaken and distressed for days afterward.

The day she arrived on campus to start up life as a student at St. Lawrence University, she felt those storms settle. The great oaks and maples stretching their branches above the green lawns of the college and town, the brick and stone buildings exuding a sense of stability, the people all knowing each other and caring about one another, all combined to make this place a haven. She decided then and there that city life had been responsible for much of her inner turmoil, and the months and years to follow only seemed to confirm that diagnosis.

She dispersed her remaining restlessness and anxiety through her writing, her novels providing the best outlet for that.

James tipped his hat to her and went on his way toward The Tick-Tock, one of the best restaurants in town, famous for their spaghetti and homemade meatballs and their Lobster Night, when they served lobsters fresh from the coast of Maine.

Pauline was tempted to follow him—her cooking was nothing to write home about—but nobly resisted the urge. Even with the supplement from her novels, money was always tight these days, and the rent was due soon.

CHAPTER TWO

The Investigation Begins

Pauline shared an apartment on the outskirts of town with her friend Sarah Jones. A black woman in a most-white region, Sarah faced enormous prejudice. Even Pauline, though she hated to remember it, had been hesitant to room with her when Sarah had first answered her advertisement for an apartment-mate.

"Oh," she had said when Sarah entered the front hall. "You're—oh."

"I'm a nurse, yes," Sarah had stated with a glint in her eye. She had removed her cap and cuffs, transforming from a practical nurse to a sweet-faced young woman with a wary twist to a mouth built for laughter. "I work at the hospital in Potsdam; just finished my shift. I hope that doesn't bother you?"

"Oh no," Pauline had stammered, too embarrassed to confess the real source of her shock. "I have no problem with, er, nurses. As long as you don't expect me to listen to your cases over the dinner table," she had surprised herself by adding.

Sarah had thrown back her head and laughed, a free, merry peal that echoed throughout the small apartment. "Fair enough! I think I can live with a newspaper columnist as well, so long as you promise never to put me in one of your columns."

From that unorthodox start, their friendship had grown into something solid and satisfying to both of them. Pauline still came up against her ingrained prejudices at times, but Sarah never hesitated to tell her when she was doing so, and Pauline worked to overcome her assumptions.

For her part, Sarah had days where she raged against "small towns and small minds," but she did her best not to hold Pauline responsible for the faults of others.

Though Sarah had not been to university, she had one of the keenest minds Pauline had ever encountered (another prejudice to overcome: thinking only those within the ivory walls of scholarship knew how to think and reason), and the two enjoyed discussing everything from current events to poetry and even modern art. Sarah was one of the few people in the world Pauline trusted with her novel-writing secret, and her analytical skills had improved many a story and unraveled many a knot in Pauline's plots.

James hadn't given her specific permission to share Ruby's story with Sarah, but Pauline trusted her friend. With any luck, Sarah might have some insight into the problem.

Sarah was already in the kitchen of their second-story apartment by the time Pauline mounted the steps and entered, hanging her hat in the small foyer and walking through to see what her friend was concocting for dinner.

"Tomato soup, I'm afraid," Sarah said, indicating the pot she was stirring. "Pay-day isn't for another few days, and the rent —,"

"I know," said Pauline, suppressing a sigh.

She could be eating well at her parents' house, or even— ghastly thought—presiding over a dinner table of her own with a husband and baby, had she followed her mother's wishes and returned to Albany after finishing her degree.

Yes, and be a miserable knotted mass of frustrated ambition and suppressed interests. What did the Scriptures say?

"Better a dinner of herbs with a friend than the fatted calf with hatred therein," she said aloud. "Or something like that."

Sarah turned from the stove, her brow wrinkling. "Isn't the fatted calf from the Prodigal Son story?"

Pauline waved such minor details away. "The idea is the same."

She moved to the counter and opened the breadbox. "One slice or two?" she asked about the Wonder bread therein.

Sarah requested one, and turned off the flame under the soup as Pauline got out plates and bowls and buttered the bread.

Over their simple meal, Pauline told Sarah of her encounter with Ruby, followed by James' shocking revelation. Sarah sniffed.

"Anonymous letters! I've experienced a few of those in my time. Cowards, that's all the people who write those are, somebody who has nothing better to do than spew hate at others but doesn't have the courage to do it publicly."

"Why would anyone send you an anonymous letter?" Pauline exclaimed. She couldn't imagine her friend living anything but a blameless life.

Sarah raised her eyebrows. "People who don't like the color of my skin, or the fact that they have to see me, or that I work in a job that involves me interacting with the likes of them."

Pauline flushed, ashamed both of the naiveté of her question and the blind prejudice of people who shared her own skin color.

"My advice to Ruby would be to ignore the letters," Sarah concluded.

"These are different, though," Pauline said, staring into her bowl of soup. "These are aimed at uncovering a secret, not saying nasty things about Ruby."

"You think there's something to them," Sarah said, watching her with a knowing eye.

Pauline raised a hand and tilted it back and forth. "James said I ought not to entertain the notion, but—well. Either way, we need to find out who's behind it. Where would be the best place to find out if a woman has been scheming or acting strangely lately?"

"Ladies Aid," Sarah said promptly. "Missionary Circle. Choir practice. Sunday School. Sewing Circle."

"Enough!" Pauline said, catching her breath on a laugh. "Why are you so much more knowledgable about gossip than I?"

"Because you are too busy writing or researching most of the time to pay attention to such things," Sarah said with a smile. "And when you are looking out for gossip, it's for your newspaper column and you can ask people directly. You don't have a sneaky mind."

Pauline wasn't sure whether this was criticism or praise. She dismissed it to focus on Sarah's suggestions.

"I am not a member of any of those groups," she said, tapping the edge of the bowl with her spoon. "By the time I join and people are familiar enough with me to talk freely, weeks or months could have passed. I need something more immediate."

Sarah reached across the small round table and gripped Pauline's wrist to stop her tapping. Pauline started, unaware she had been doing so.

"The Episcopal Ladies Sewing Circle meets tomorrow, doesn't it? All you have to do is telephone Mrs. Hansen this evening and tell her you'd like to attend. She might think it odd, but nobody would raise an eyebrow at it. At most, they'd feel smug that at last you are starting to see the value in their groups and gatherings."

Pauline narrowed her eyes. "The Sewing Circle, really? After how they treated you?"

She had agreed to go once last year, when Sarah wanted to join but didn't feel comfortable attending on her own. Though nobody had demanded outright Sarah leave, the cold shoulders, the snubs, the whispering behind hands, had left Pauline in a rage, vowing never to attend another meeting so long as she lived.

Sarah had taken the rejection more philosophically, finding other societal outcasts and forming a private Sewing Club with them instead.

Sarah's smile turned mischievous. "Think of it this way. With your sewing abilities, it'll probably be more punishment for them to have you there than not. They'll be so focused on your mangled seams that they won't even notice if your questions are odd!"

Pauline couldn't help but laugh. It was undeniable that while Sarah could transform a dress into a completely new garment overnight, Pauline could not so much as stitch a smooth buttonhole.

"I do appreciate domestic skills," she said ruefully. "I just can't seem to cultivate any of them."

"It's decided, then," Sarah said. She looked down at the rim of orange circling the inside of her empty bowl. "Perhaps you can tuck some snacks into your bag to bring home, as well."

CHAPTER THREE

Sewing Circle Clues

Sarah had the early shift at the hospital next day, so she was out of the apartment by the time Pauline was up and about. Though Pauline longed to be one of those people who rose blithely with the sun each day, without the impetus of an early class or an outside job to propel her she rarely managed to crack her eyes open before eight o'clock.

After eating a spartan breakfast of a boiled egg, one slice of toast, and the invaluable cup of coffee to accompany it, Pauline did her share of tidying: she washed the few dishes left from the morning meal, ran the carpet sweeper over the floors, and dusted the furniture and bookshelves. These chores out of the way, she sat down at her typewriter to get in some editing before leaving for the Sewing Circle.

It was no good. She couldn't concentrate on the perils and triumphs of her dashing heroine Emma, who in this chapter was supposed to be trekking through the desert in search of her kidnapped niece and nephew, and instead kept getting herself mired in a swamp of grammatical errors and plot holes.

Rather than focusing on the task at hand, Pauline found herself staring out the window into the branches of the flaming maple tree growing close by their building and pondering the mysterious anonymous letters.

She could accept James' dictum that there were people out there in the world who would send anonymous letters for the thrill of it. She could even accept that there were such people in this village, distasteful as the notion was. She relied on Canton to be kinder and gentler than Albany or any large city, but she knew there were hate-filled and loathsome people here as well as there. She couldn't imagine any of her neighbors, friends, or acquaintances doing such a thing, but everyone had a private life, secrets they wouldn't share with anyone.

Look at her! She held her novel-writing tightly to her chest. Surely others had joys and sorrows they refused to reveal as well.

Much as she hated to think there was somebody—someone she might know, might even see today at the Sewing Circle— who took pleasure in bringing misery to Ruby, she still couldn't understand why they would use Bob's death. There had to be more recent rumors one could concoct. Was it that Bob's death was the cruelest thing they could think of? But sending her nasty notes about Jeremy, or her relationship with James, or ... well, Pauline could think of a hundred small, spiteful things one could say if one truly wanted nothing more than to spread vitriol.

Granted, not every person had her imagination, but even so.

Pauline leaned back as best she could in her upright wooden chair, eyes still absently fixed on a stout grey squirrel rummaging for seeds in the maple tree, and tried to remember what she could about Bob's death.

Four years ago, Pauline had been two years out of college, struggling to make ends meet. She hadn't secured her job as a newspaper columnist then, getting by with the occasional feature or "domestic" article. Her novel writing had begun around then, stirred on by desperation and the feeling that "anyone can write this kind of trash."

She had met Bob and Ruby at the big Episcopal church they all attended, but she hadn't known either of them well when he died. The details of his accident were hazy. All she could remember for certain was that he had fallen into the Grasse River from the third-story window of the grist mill, hit his head on a submerged rock, and drowned before help could arrive.

Tragic—and Mr. Wharton, the mill owner, had been chastised for not having proper safety railings and window bars in place to prevent such things—but there had been no hint of foul play. Bob was a courteous, well-spoken, gentle man; Pauline couldn't imagine anyone wanting to kill him.

Unless—suppose he had known something dreadful about somebody, so that person killed him to keep it a secret. Or maybe there was a man who had always been in love with Ruby, and he killed Bob out of jealousy. Or maybe it was a childhood squabble that had festered for years, leading a person to kill out of sheer hatred. Or—

Pauline snorted softly and got to her feet. She had been reading too many of her own works. People might kill for those sorts of reasons in lurid adventure novels, but not in sensible, everyday life.

She checked her appearance in the mirror over the mantel to

make sure her dark hair was smooth and tidy in its low bun before putting on her jacket and hat to walk to the church. The Sewing Circle met in one of the basement rooms to avoid putting undue strain on anyone's hospitality. In these economically challenged times, it was a bit much to ask someone to host twelve to twenty women in her home once a month, eating up her food and dirtying her furniture and floors.

This way, a few different ladies could each bring food to share with the group and others could help sweep and tidy after they finished, and nobody had to bear the brunt of the cost and effort alone. It did mean for a less homey atmosphere, but alas, times changed and people changed with them.

The basement of the stone church was chilly as always, and Pauline shivered inside her plain brown broadcloth suit. She wished she could have worn her thick, hand-knitted sweater from Aunt Mildred, but for an occasion such as this, looking proper was more important than warmth. There was only so much she could get away with as an eccentric young writer.

She would have to wait until she was an eccentric *elderly* writer for the rest of it.

Turning a corner after the last flight of uncarpeted stairs, she entered the large, well-lit room filled with ladies and sewing material of all types and descriptions. Pauline's heart sank as a perfumed and powdered Lucy Westin rushed up to her, gushing about her latest "piece" in the *Times* and pressing a frilly white baby dress on her—

"So sweet, you know, so dainty and delicate for some neglected little love."

Here Miss Westin stopped and sighed, her blue eyes rounded and mournful.

Pauline smiled politely. "Actually, I'd prefer something with plain stitching," she said.

She caught the flash of malice in Miss Westin's face, a sense of satisfaction as Mrs. Hansen hustled Pauline away and handed her a plain woolen blanket to be hemmed. Why?

Understanding came a moment later. Miss Westin had wanted to point out Pauline's inadequacy with a needle, and felt she had succeeded by making Pauline admit fancy stitchery was beyond her. That it hadn't bothered Pauline in the slightest did not matter in the least to her.

Such pettiness! Pauline nodded in genuine gratitude to Mrs. Hansen and settled in between two stout matrons, senses alert to the first chance to turn the tide of gossip toward anonymous letters, Ruby Ferris, or mysterious deaths.

At first, the chat was solely about who was seeing whom, who was about to give birth, and whose husbands had recently lost their jobs. Pauline was nearly ready to scream with frustration before at last one woman commented,

"Such a pity about Ellis Crawford. Only forty years old, and dead of pneumonia. Doesn't seem right."

They all sighed in agreement. Pauline let the conversation linger on Ellis, his family, and their prospects now before casually inserting a comment of her own.

"We don't get too many deaths of that sort—I mean, men of that age—around here, thankfully. Why I think the last one was ..." She pretended to think about it. "Bob Ferris, wasn't it?"

That sparked a lively debate as to how many people had died in between Bob and Ellis, before Pauline was able to speak again.

"Of course, they aren't exactly alike. Poor Mr. Crawford died of illness, while Bob's death was sudden and shocking. Some might even call it mysterious."

Mrs. Hansen sniffed. "Nothing mysterious about that. Mr. Wharton was not keeping the mill in good condition, and Bob paid the price." A pinched look settled on her plump face. "It seems Mr. Wharton is getting his comeuppance now, though. Have you heard that the mill might close? Not enough work to keep them in business."

Exclamations arose around the room. It seemed none of the ladies had heard that particular rumor.

"That's horrible," said one of the matrons beside Pauline. "What will his workers do?"

"Same as everyone else who has been laid off in the last few years—the best they can," said Mrs. Hansen.

"I am sorry for them, but not for Andrew Wharton," said another woman. "He's been a mean, tight-fisted boss from the beginning. It serves him right to go under now."

Pauline made a mental note. Andrew Wharton was unlikely to be the letter-writer, but could he have been a murderer? What if he and Bob had gotten into a fight? Perhaps he'd threatened to cut Bob's wages, or even talked about letting him go, and Bob had lost his temper (for even the gentlest of men might turn ugly at such a prospect), swung at him, Wharton had defended himself and knocked Bob out the window. A passer-by could have seen it and ...

But here Pauline's imagination failed her. Why this hypothetical person would not have reported it to the police was beyond her. Could somebody have seen Wharton from the road below, anyway?

Or wait! Maybe it was another worker who witnessed it from inside the mill, and he was afraid of losing his own job if he ratted on the boss, so he kept quiet. Only now he was in danger of losing his job because of the mill closure, so he had nothing to lose. He felt too guilty to tell the police after all this time, so he wrote to Ruby in hopes that the police would investigate the case and discover the truth without him having to be involved.

A neat case. Pauline was proud of it. She determined to

present it to James at the first opportunity.

The circle broke for coffee and snacks, Pauline smiling as she remembered Sarah's charge to bring some home. She'd do her best, but only if she could sneak them into her bag without anyone noticing.

This was not that moment, as Lucy Westin oozed up to her.

"What made you say that about Bob's death being mysterious, Miss Gray?" she asked.

Pauline assumed a careless air. "Oh, I don't know. I suppose it's my newspaper training, always looking for a story. Nobody saw him fall, did they?"

Miss Westin's eyes rounded. "Do you think he was *pushed*? Or that he jumped, like those bankers we read about in the city papers?"

Pauline felt a frisson of alarm. She hadn't meant to start this sort of speculation!

"Goodness, when you say it like that it does sound nonsensical," she laughed. "Of course Bob wouldn't jump. Nor can I imagine anyone wanting to push him. I'm not sure what sort of mystery I was imagining, but now we're talking about it, I realize it had to have been an accident."

Miss Westin looked unusually thoughtful. "I don't know, I'm sure. There were those who said he regretted marrying Ruby. His older sister Iris kept house for him before he and Ruby married, and stayed with them a few months after until she moved out to the boarding house. She and Ruby hated each other. They fought constantly, until Bob was fed up with the both of them and paid Iris's board at Mrs. Johnson's just to keep them apart."

"A man doesn't kill himself over his wife and sister squabbling, especially years later," Pauline said.

She made another mental note all the same. Could Iris be

the one writing to Ruby, one final way of hurting the sister-in-law she loathed? Perhaps she, in some twisted way, blamed Ruby for Bob's death and wanted to make her suffer for it.

Another theory to bring to James's attention, though it was ugly enough she almost wished she hadn't thought of it. Thinking about that sort of malice made her stomach twist and her muscles clench.

"I suppose not," Miss Westin said. "Not that you or I have any experience in such matters!" Her laugh rang shrilly in Pauline's ears.

It was common knowledge that Lucy Westin hated her single status as much as Pauline enjoyed hers. Pauline pitied her, but she couldn't like her. It had nothing to do with Miss Westin's desperation for a husband and everything to do with her insincerity. You never could trust her; she said sweet things to your face but always with a hidden sting in them.

Pauline almost wished they could pin the letters on her, but she doubted even Miss Westin would go that far to spread a nasty rumor. She preferred face-to-face gossip.

"Certainly Iris Ferris has gotten all the more sour since her brother's death. There really seems to be only one person who didn't regret his passing," Miss Westin mused now.

Pauline sharpened her ears. "Oh?"

She knew better than to trust Miss Westin, but however false her claim, it might give Pauline a clue in the right direction.

"Oh well, I shouldn't gossip about such things. Only everyone knows that John Kitteredge has been in love with Ruby Ferris since they were in grade school together."

"Yet he and Ruby aren't together now," Pauline pointed out.

Lucy Westin shrugged. "I suppose James Richardson got there first." She raised her eyebrows.

To respond with the insistence that she and James were only friends would fuel the fire of Miss Westin's insinuations. "James and Ruby are so well suited to each other," Pauline said cheerfully instead.

Miss Westin sighed and moved on to other victims, leaving Pauline inclined to dismiss her words, but holding John Kitteredge in reserve in case there should be a shred of truth in them.

She resolved to find out if he really had been in love with Ruby and if he was the kind of man to kill out of passion.

She loudly praised the quality of the homemade goodies to Mrs. Hansen, saying how much she wished she could bake half so well as all the ladies there. As she had hoped, this spurred an instant offer of recipes, all to be written as soon as the ladies returned home and delivered at the next Sewing Circle. It didn't give Pauline handwriting samples for comparison right now, but it was a promising start.

The group resumed their sewing after that, and the meeting ended without any more revelations. Pauline felt it had not been a waste, especially as Mrs. Hansen took her aside afterward and pressed a platter of cookies and muffins on her.

"To take back and share with Miss Jones," she said. "I, er, do wish she could join us on these occasions."

A nicely ambiguous statement, conveying as much the impression that Sarah couldn't come because of her work schedule as because of society's prejudices. Pauline would have preferred an outright apology for the treatment Sarah received, but at least Mrs. Hansen was making an effort.

Leaving the church building with plate in hand, Pauline sifted through everything she had heard, forming two columns in her mind to write out as soon as she got home. One column was labeled "murderer," and in it were Andrew Wharton and

John Kitteredge.

The other column was "letter-writer," and on it were Iris Ferris and unknown mill worker.

Mulling things over, Pauline didn't notice the man approaching until he nearly ran her over. They both stopped, startled by the near-collision.

"Oh!" Pauline straightened her hat. "I'm so sorry, I didn't even see you coming."

"My fault," he said. The man in question was short and burly, with well-muscled arms and broad shoulders, brown hair and eyes, and a well-defined chin. He looked vaguely familiar, but Pauline couldn't quite place him. "Did I hurt you?"

"Not at all," she assured him. She gave up her attempt to recognize him and asked outright, "Do I know you? I'm so sorry, I'm terrible at remembering faces."

He managed a smile, which lightened his face considerably. She hadn't realized how dour he looked until that smile briefly lit his features.

"Dan Harwood. We've seen each other a few places, but I don't think we've ever been introduced. I know who you are, though: you're P. Gray, the woman newspaper writer."

Pauline admitted her identity. Then she placed Mr. Harwood.

No wonder she hadn't recognized him: the last time she'd seen him was at Bob Ferris's funeral four years previously. Perhaps he would have a clue as to what had happened that day at the mill!

She was racking her brains trying to figure out a subtle way to ask him when he spoke again.

"Are you working on a story right now? Is that what distracted you?"

"I—yes," she said on the impulse of the moment. "I'm

thinking of a piece on local businesses. I want to write something about the grist mill. You work there, don't you, Mr. Harwood? I don't suppose you could give me a quote?"

It was a pathetic way to introduce the topic of Bob's death, but it was the best she could do spur of the moment.

His face darkened. "The mill! Not much point in including that in your piece, unless you want to talk about businesses that shut down and put all their employees out of work after years and years of faithful service."

"Oh dear," said Pauline inadequately. Clearly the rumor about the mill closing wasn't unsubstantiated gossip. No wonder Mr. Harwood was so upset he nearly ran her down. "I'm so sorry."

He made a visible effort to calm down. "Not your fault. Sorry, Miss Gray." He attempted another smile, this one less successful than the first. "Have a nice day. Good luck on your story."

He stepped around her, leaving Pauline to make her way back to the apartment without any other untoward encounters. She dropped off the snacks with a note stating: *Mrs. H's attempt at an apology to you*, and turned right around and left again, wishing she still had her old bicycle.

Walking all over the village kept her in good trim, no doubt, but it was wearing on shoe leather.

CHAPTER FOUR

Murder!

Pauline chose to come the back way into town rather than walking past the churches and the park, and the allure of the Canton Free Library. Many a day had she come out of browsing through the library stacks to blink in the bright sunshine and take her book (or books) to sit under a tree in the park and finish reading. No such joys today, alas.

She came out onto Main Street higher up than that dangerous turn to the library, heading once more for the Town Hall. James Richardson intercepted her before she arrived.

"Pauline! What are you doing?"

Pauline had never seen James look so distressed. His usually crisply curling hair was untidy and mussed beneath his uniform cap; his eyes were restless and his face shadowed.

"Coming to see you," she said, surprised both by his appearance and his tone. "I have some theories about those letters."

He exhaled loudly. "Too late."

"What?" Indignation rose in Pauline's breast. Had she wasted an entire morning at the Sewing Circle for nothing? "You caught the culprit?"

James's face turned grim. "Someone did."

Pauline's stomach lurched, though she hardly knew why. "What?" she said again.

James took her arm and led her closer to the buildings lining the street so pedestrians could get past them. He lowered his voice. "Do you know Jemima Root?"

Pauline frowned in concentration. The name didn't bring a face to mind. "Possibly, but if so, not well."

"It doesn't matter. She's one of the old maids who proliferate all small villages. Too nosy for her own good, a little spiteful, probably bitter about never getting married."

Despite the situation, Pauline leveled him with a gimlet stare. "*Really*, James."

"Sorry. I shouldn't say things like that about her now, God knows."

"You mean …?"

"She was murdered this morning."

The words were blunt, unforgiving. Pauline rested her hand on the warm brick of the shop front as the world spun around her. A familiar cloud of stomach-clenching black nausea rose in her stomach.

"I found some unfinished letters when I examined the scene," James went on, his voice harsh and guttural. "They were addressed to Ruby, same handwriting and everything. She's—she was—the letter writer. And either she wrote a letter to someone who took it very badly, or what she wrote was the truth and Bob's murderer finished her off as well."

Pauline had a hold of herself now, forcing the anxiety into a box in the back of her mind until she could write her way through it later.

Murder was an ugly thing, but she was a scholar, and she would not let emotions get in the way of facing facts.

"In that case, I have a few suspects for you," she said.

"No," James said.

Pauline blinked her dark brown eyes at him a few times. "I beg your pardon?"

"This is beyond a Poison Pen. This is murder, Pauline. It's far too dangerous for you to be mixed up in. I wish I'd never told you about the letters in the first place!"

"What if I had evidence in the case? Would you tell me to run along home and not trouble over it because it might be dangerous?"

"This isn't evidence. It's speculation."

Outrage swelled in Pauline. She rose to her full height, as opposed to the scholarly slouch she normally adopted, a side-effect of too much time spent hunched over a desk. "You don't want to hear my suspects and deductions? Even if my 'speculation' could help you catch the murderer? Even if all I do is tell you my observations and then walk away?"

James shook his head. "I know you, Pauline. You can't walk away from your own curiosity. You'd tell me, and when I expressed doubt you'd be determined to prove yourself, so you'd keep digging and ferreting around, and the next thing you know I'd have your dead body on my hands as well."

There were several fallacies in that statement, from the assumption that he would disbelieve her to the idea that the murderer would find her even if she was on the wrong trail, but Pauline wouldn't pick apart his logic now.

"What makes you think I'll be any more docile if you refuse to listen to me at all? Aren't I far more likely to dig around and get into trouble to prove myself right if you won't listen to me?"

James groaned. "A curse on all strong-minded women!" he said, looking up at the cloudless sky. He lowered his gaze to Pauline's stubborn face. "Very well. But not here, and not now."

"Do you want me to come make a statement?" she asked tartly.

He didn't appear amused. "I'll stop by this evening after I get off duty and listen to your theories then. If you promise me that will be an end to it!"

"I can't promise I won't keep thinking about it," she said. "But theoretical speculation only. I won't go around looking for trouble, I promise."

She wanted to see justice done, but she wasn't a trained investigator, and as much as she loathed James's over-protective and outdated attitude toward women, he had a point. She was not equipped to physically confront a murderer—not, she added to herself, because she was a woman, but because she lived far too sedentary a lifestyle. Sitting and thinking was much more her style.

"I'll take what I can get," he said grimly. "See you this evening."

Left alone on the busy street, Pauline strove to order her thoughts.

Murder—in Canton. This was no long-past "perhaps" as with Bob's death, or far-off violence one read about in the papers. This was real, and present, and the fact that she could not picture the dead woman's face made it all the more horrible. She ought to have known her. They were neighbors. She ought to be able to mourn her.

Ahead of her, Sarah exited Newberry's with a small woven bag over one arm, dressed in a pretty flowered frock now her nursing shift was done. Glad for the distraction, Pauline called her name and hurried forward to join her.

"We needed more soap, and ..." the other woman's voice trailed off as she took in Pauline's face. "Good heavens. What happened?"

In a low voice, Pauline told her the news. Sarah's lips tightened.

"I see," she said.

"James is coming over this evening so we can talk through my list of suspects and theories," Pauline said.

"Good," said Sarah, setting a faster pace back toward the apartment on Pleasant St. "Because this isn't fun anymore. Murder isn't a game, after all."

CHAPTER FIVE

Consultations

James stretched out his long legs before the fireplace, swirling his tumbler of whiskey thoughtfully. He seemed to take up twice as much space in their small living room than he really did, simply by virtue of being a man. Neither Sarah nor Pauline was in the habit of bringing young men home.

James seemed comfortable enough there, slouched in the best armchair, staring into the flickering red and gold flames. Pauline was curled up on the hearthrug, with Sarah occupying the other armchair.

Pauline also had whiskey; Sarah didn't care for the taste and therefore nursed a glass of orange juice.

"I shouldn't be indulging, you know," James said at last,

taking another sip. "Not as a law enforcement officer."

"I'm not selling it or buying it," Pauline said, her voice a tad prim. "I inherited it from my grandfather. And you're not here as a police officer, you're here as a friend."

"True," James conceded. He sat up a little straighter with a grin. "Still, best to destroy the evidence, eh?" He swallowed the last of what was in his glass and set it down on the side table with a clink. "Let's hear what you have to say about the Root case."

Pauline tore her mind away from Prohibition. She wasn't a hard drinker by any stretch of the imagination, but from her mother's father she had learned to appreciate fine wines and other liquors. Word was that President Roosevelt was going to overturn Prohibition as early as this winter. The sooner the better, said Pauline. Grandfather's stock was dwindling, and she was tired of having to hide her enjoyment of the occasional glass from her more respectable neighbors.

Without looking at James for fear of seeing derision at her deductions and suppositions, she laid out for him the reasons for her two suspects in the case of Bob's death. She wrapped up by saying she had at first wondered if Iris Ferris was the Poison Pen, writing to Ruby out of empty spite, but that theory was shattered in light of Jemima Root's authorship.

A brief silence hung over the room as she finished. Sarah stood up and switched on a few more lamps to dispel the gloom. In the homey yellow light spilling from beneath their fringed shades, James stirred himself to speak.

"I'd be drummed out of the force if I suggested we investigate Andrew Wharton. He's one of the richest men in St. Lawrence County! Not that that means much, compared with New York City," he added in a bitter aside, the lament common to every rural dweller forced to live in the shadow of that shining metropolis. "And John Kitteredge ... it's weak, Pauline. He never made any move to pursue Ruby after Bob's death, and he's certainly never shown any enmity toward me."

"Perhaps he was horrified by what he did to Bob and couldn't follow through on it," Sarah suggested in her soft voice.

James shook his head. "In my experience—well, this is my first murder, but from what I've learned in training and from older officers, if a man works himself up to commit murder, he's not going to shy away from taking advantage of it afterward."

Pauline leaned forward, locking her arms around her updrawn knees. "But what if it was an impulse of the moment? Giving way to the overpowering emotion of jealousy, only to be horror-stricken the moment it's done? He might not even have meant it as murder—if Bob hadn't hit his head he might well have survived that fall."

James laughed. "What a description! You should be writing novels, not just newspaper features."

She was glad the fire made an excuse for her cheeks to grow hot.

"So you really think Kitteredge did it?"

"I don't know," she said frankly. "I think Wharton is more likely, but when I really stop and think about it, it seems ridiculous that it could have been anything but an accident. It seems ridiculous that Jemima Root could have been murdered, too, yet here we are."

"It is hard to picture a murderer in our little community," James agreed. "The chief is of the opinion the letters were the result of her being a repressed spinster—I know it's awful, Pauline, you needn't snort at me like that—rather than truth, and he's looking for other recipients, one of whom might have killed her for her insinuations. He wouldn't consider Bob's death as a possible murder."

"Shouldn't the police want to look at every possibility, as

well as every suspect?" Sarah asked. "Instead of avoiding Andrew Wharton, avoiding the possibility of two murders, avoiding anything too unpleasant that isn't right under his nose and demanding attention?"

"It's not entirely his fault," James said. "He wants to solve it quickly, before the city newspapers get a hold of it and the state police decide we can't handle it ourselves. If I brought him hard evidence, he'd investigate even Andrew Wharton. He does have a point: it is far more likely Miss Root sent out letters to many people and someone attacked her for it. The only reason I'm pursuing the possibility of Bob being murdered and Miss Root's death covering it up is because I am the lowest man on this case. Everyone else is investigating the more plausible lines; this out-there notion is all that's left for me. Besides, if someone *did* kill Bob, I owe it to Ruby to find out."

The firelight flickering over the amber whiskey left in the bottom of her tumbler started a new train of thought for Pauline. She unwound her arms from around her knees and sat up straighter. "What if it wasn't personal?"

"What do you mean?"

"We're assuming someone killed Bob because of who he was, but what if he was simply in the wrong place at the wrong time? What if he saw or heard something he wasn't supposed to?"

James groaned. "Then it could be anyone who did it!"

"No, because it would still have to be someone who had access to the third floor of the mill," Pauline said. "And I wasn't thinking in vague terms. James, are there any smugglers in Canton?"

She'd startled him. He froze in his chair, eyes wide.

"James?"

He relaxed again. "Sorry. I—you took me aback. Before Miss

Root's murder, our biggest focus in the forces across the county has been on clearing out a smuggler's ring that's been operating in this area for the last five years or so. We know they're based in the Thousand Islands. The whiskey they bring across the St. Lawrence River from Canada goes to New York City, but there's a transfer station in one of the small towns hereabouts, we don't know which one. It's one of the reasons the chief wants this murder solved quickly, so we can get back to the smuggling problem."

"I hardly think smuggling is more important than a murderer," said Pauline.

"Not more important, no, but you have to understand, we're part of a joint operation between village police departments and the state troopers, and it's been going on for a long time. The chief feels we'd be letting down all the other people involved if we dropped out for a more localized issue."

"But what if they are connected?" Sarah asked. "Pauline, you think Bob might have seen a smuggler in action and been killed to prevent him talking to the police?"

"Not likely—they don't tend toward violence—but more plausible than Wharton," said James. "If one of Bob's fellow workers was a smuggler on the side, and Bob saw or heard something some night along the banks of the St. Lawrence or coming into town ... yes, I could see a man panicking and killing him to keep that from coming to light. Most folk around here look the other way when it comes to smuggling, but Bob was an upstanding citizen. He might not have been willing to let it be."

Or perhaps, Pauline speculated, Bob didn't care, but the smuggler offered him a bribe to keep quiet, and Bob was so furious at the implied stain on his honor that he swore he would go to the police that very day, and so the man had to kill him.

But who would it be? Who amidst the mill employees might

be smuggling on the side? Pauline didn't know of anyone in town whose style of living was higher than his income allowed.

Sarah tapped her fingers against the arm of her chair. "The other person I think we should keep in mind is Iris Ferris. We now know she wasn't the Poison Pen, but how angry was she at her brother for marrying Ruby and robbing her of her position and home? What if she pushed him?"

"She didn't work at the mill," Pauline objected.

"Besides, she loved Bob," James said. "It was Ruby she hated. And it's not as though they kicked her out or left her penniless. She was no longer Bob's chief confidante and housekeeper, but they would have let her keep living with them. It was her own choice to move to the boarding house and take a job."

Pauline and Sarah's eyes met above James's head. No man could ever truly understand the thwarted fury of a woman who had her entire value taken away in one fell swoop by another woman. Who would want to live on charity in the house where she had once ruled? No, if it weren't for the fact that Iris would have no reason to be at the mill when Bob was killed, Pauline would consider her a likely subject.

"She might have brought him lunch or something," Sarah persisted.

Pauline snapped her fingers. "That's it! Then he could have thoughtlessly told her that Ruby had already packed him one, and she, consumed by jealousy and bitterness, pushed him with all her strength, not intending death but helpless to stop it once he fell out the open window and landed on that rock. In a moment of weakness she confessed her crime to Jemima Root, who became determined to see justice done and so wrote to Ruby. When Iris found out she had to kill again, not out of anger this time, but for her own safety."

James's laughter broke the hush that filled the room after Pauline finished. "I'll say it again, you ought to be writing for the talkies! You could call it, oh, I don't know, *The Perils of Pauline*?" He winked.

"Ha ha," Pauline said flatly.

Sarah hurried to speak. "You bring up a good point we haven't considered yet. How *did* Miss Root find out about Bob's murder? Where did she get her information?"

James stood up and stretched, his fair hair nearly brushing the ceiling. "I'll look into our suspects as discreetly as possible and try to find out if Miss Root was anywhere near the mill that day to see something incriminating or if, as Pauline so colorfully speculated, someone confessed to her and then regretted it afterward. I'll also look into any possible links between the mill and the smuggling ring. Pauline, Miss Jones, if your speculations lead to any other theories, I'm happy to hear them. But remember your promise, Pauline—no active investigating!"

Pauline rose to her feet as well, brushing down her skirt as she stood. "I remember," she said.

She preferred the emotional distance provided by treating this as an intellectual exercise, which immediately led her to suspect her own motives in agreeing so promptly. Was it fair to isolate herself so from the matter? And how much further could she pursue her investigation without talking to people?

Did casual chit-chat, such as this morning at the Sewing Circle, count as "active investigation?" She should have made James clarify, but he had already put on his hat and coat and bid them goodnight.

Pauline closed the door on the frosty, starlit night, and returned to her seat by the fire.

Sarah picked up the skirt she'd been hemming before James's arrival and said, "You know, you are a newspaper writer. What was that line you fed Mr. Harwood this morning?"

"You mean about me working on a story about local businesses?"

Sarah nodded. "You could always arrange an interview with Mr. Wharton about the mill; maybe even talk to some of the other employees. You could even put an angle on it about the need to support local businesses so they stay open and continue to provide jobs for our towns."

Pauline was tempted. "I promised James I wouldn't interfere."

"If you keep yourself strictly to newspaper questions, I hardly see that as interfering," Sarah said, a demure smile playing about her mouth. "Your speculations as a result of those questions is entirely your own affair."

It felt like splitting hairs. On the other hand, that was exactly the sort of story the *Times* appreciated from her, and the promotion of a local business, especially one that employed so many people in the county, was a good thing in this troubled time.

If James questioned her about it later, she could truthfully tell him it was a legitimate story inspired by their investigation, not an excuse.

Her conscience was still mildly troubled, but she decided she was being squeamish and selfish, and silenced it.

"Do you suppose it is too late to call Mr. Wharton and ask for an interview tomorrow at the mill?" she asked.

Sarah's smile turned vulpine. "Not at all."

CHAPTER SIX

At the Mill

At precisely 10:00 the next morning, Pauline presented herself at the front entrance to the Wharton Grist Mill. Rather than spend her entire morning walking the six miles from Canton to the mill, Pauline had borrowed a bicycle from a St. Lawrence University student, telling herself once again she really needed to buy a new one for herself with her next royalty check

She had given away the rusty, rickety old thing she had used while a student herself as soon as she'd signed her first book contract. She'd felt it beneath her dignity to get around on such an ancient contraption. With a few more years under her belt now, she wished she had not been so eagerly imprudent.

Still, Jean-Paul wouldn't have passed his freshman English

classes without her tutoring last year, so he owed her a favor. Loaning her his bicycle for the day hardly put a dent in that, especially as he'd painted it bright red, making it (and its rider) dreadfully conspicuous.

Pauline had enjoyed the ride, the sharp air making her cheeks tingle and filling her lungs with life, the pageant of the trees on either side of the road dazzling her eyes every time she looked, the sound of Canada geese honking overhead as they flew south striking an adventurous chord in her soul. As she drew closer to the mill, she could see and hear the Grasse River burbling placidly away on her left. Some of the dark emotions that had been troubling her ever since learning about the anonymous letters eased out under the influence of that ride.

Pauline's family occasionally wrote asking when she was going to tire of her "rusticating lifestyle" and return to "real life" in Albany. *Never*, she told them. Days like this only confirmed her resolve. Whatever troubles might plague this town, it was still the place where she felt the most at home.

Dan Harwood met her at the entrance to the mill and told her Mr. Wharton was awaiting her in his office. Following him through the old stone building, weaving her careful way around the various pulleys, wooden shafts, stones, and sacks, coughing a little at all the dust in the air, glancing at the blank, empty faces of the workers, shivering at a chill in the air that had nothing to do with the actual temperature of the place, Pauline searched for something polite to say to Mr. Harwood.

He saved her the difficulty. "Miss Gray, would you—do you mind—could you not say anything to Mr. Wharton about seeing me yesterday?"

"Certainly," Pauline began in surprise.

He hurried into further explanation, eyes glancing around he building as he spoke. "I was supposed to be picking up supplies at the train station, you see, but Mr. Wharton had just announced about the mill shutting down and I was upset, and I had to walk around town to cool off enough to return to work. Mr. Wharton, he wouldn't understand, and if he fires me for shirking tasks I'll be out of a job that much sooner, and have that much of a harder time finding some other work."

A pang of pity smote Pauline's heart. How awful to feel so trapped and desperate for even a few more days of work. She didn't know much about Dan, but she knew there was an old Mrs. Harwood and at least three younger siblings.

What kind of a world were they living in, where a hardworking, honest man couldn't even be guaranteed the opportunity to feed his mother and younger siblings? She felt almost ashamed of her own relative ease. She was not wealthy, but her two writing jobs brought in enough income for her to never fear losing her home. Even if Sarah married or moved on, Pauline would simply have to move to a smaller and less comfortable apartment; she wouldn't have to sleep on the streets. She might not eat caviar and *fois gras*, but she had three meals a day, filling if not fancy.

Pauline's voice was often called brusque by people who did not care for her, so she consciously modulated it to a gentler tone to respond. "Of course, Mr. Harwood. I won't tell a soul. I see nothing wrong in needing to clear one's head after such distressing news, and if Mr. Wharton does, he shan't hear about it from me."

The tension in those broad shoulders eased slightly. "Thank you, Miss Gray."

By now, they had arrived at the small inner office belonging to Mr. Wharton. Dan knocked, and that smooth tenor Pauline had heard over the telephone last night rang out.

"What is it?"

"Miss Gray from the *Times*, Mr. Wharton," Dan called back.

The door opened and there he stood, the mill owner himself in all his sleekly polished glory. Pauline couldn't help but compare his aura of well-being and comfort to the dull hopelessness of his employees.

"Ah, Miss Gray!" he boomed, taking both her hands in his. Another count against him—had she been a male reporter, he would have shaken her hand. "So pleased you could come. Thank you Harwood, that will be all," he added in an abrupt aside.

Dan ducked his head, mumbled something, and left them. Mr. Wharton drew Pauline into his bright, well-lit office, closing the door behind her.

"I apologize for that. Harwood needs someone on him at all times or he's useless. My regular foreman is not in today. Harwood is filling in for him, but he's rough around the edges." He flashed a smile. "This is all off the record, of course."

"Of course," Pauline said, burying her dislike of him under a layer of professionalism.

He seated himself behind his massive oak desk, so tidy on its surface Pauline suspected it was never actually used, and waved her to a chair opposite. Pauline drew her skirts around her, sat down, and pulled her notepad and pencil out of her handbag.

"Tell me, Mr. Wharton, how long has this grist mill been operating?"

The interview was underway. Pauline was surprised to hear it was not a family business; Mr. Wharton had bought it from its previous owner twenty years ago and had striven to increase its output and efficiency after that owner had let it fall into disrepair. It was a larger operation than many small-town mills, one reason why its closure was so devastating to the town.

She had to grudgingly admit he was not perhaps as bad as she wanted him to be when he spoke of all the modern improvements he had brought in, how he had wired it for electricity a few years ago, and the efforts he had made to improve working conditions and pay rate.

"It was a risk, but it would have paid off were it not for that wretched stock market crash and everything that's followed," he said, dropping his air of bonhomie and showing her a glimpse of the shrewd businessman underneath. "It would have been better for everyone—the employees, the town, the customers ..."

"And yourself?" Pauline suggested sweetly.

He laughed and leaned back in his chair, toying with a fountain pen. "Naturally! I am a businessman, not a philanthropist." He sighed, looking around the bookshelves living the office walls and the one small window showing the rushing waters of the Grasse outside. "And now it will all go away."

"Is there any way the mill can be saved?" Pauline asked. Despite his practiced patter, her sympathy was still more for the employees than their boss.

He shook his balding head. "We went through a bad patch a few years ago where things were touch and go. I don't need to tell you how hard it is to keep a thriving business in rural areas in this day and age, I'm sure."

"No," she agreed. "That's one of the reasons I'm doing this feature, in hopes of bringing attention to the plight of rural towns and small businesses." The phrase rolled glibly off her tongue due to having practiced it on her way over. She'd thought it might come in handy.

"I had to lay off about a third of my workers and cut back on operations, but we survived and I dared to hope we were through the worst of it. I had even started thinking of re-hiring some of my old employees. Now, though ..." He shook his head. "If there's a way out, I can't see it."

Pauline frowned and closed her notepad. This was not something she could put in the article, but her insatiable curiosity prompted her to ask,

"What about a business partner? Or give your employees a share in the business, make them more invested in it?" She motioned vaguely in the direction of the door. "Your foreman, perhaps, or Mr. Harwood?"

"Not a bad thought, Miss Gray. You clearly have some experience in these matters. Learned from your father, perhaps?" He raised his eyebrows, but she did not respond to the invitation. Her family was no one's business.

After a moment, he continued. "Unfortunately, workers like Harwood never make good bosses. They can't see beyond their immediate needs. As for my foreman ... well, Kitteredge is a decent fellow, but he doesn't have the passion for this place I'd need in a partner. If Bob Ferris hadn't died, now, he would have made a good partner. I had originally planned on making him my foreman when the old one retired, in fact, but then there was that ghastly accident. Harwood was the only employee with the seniority, and Kitteredge the only one with the abilities. I gave him the position and Harwood a raise, but neither of them have proved much use."

He rubbed his face with a pink silk handkerchief. "What a time that was! The accident happened the same month I was having to shrink the staff and cut back on our operations. I had people accusing me of criminal negligence, former employees threatening to burn my house, people talking of boycotting the mill, a potential investigation by the state police, everything." He gave her a weary smile, tucking the hanky back into his pocket. "Seems a mite unfair to have weathered all that only to lose it now, doesn't it?"

Pauline had no time for pity. He had given her the perfect opportunity to talk about Bob. "Oh yes, then," she said, nodding. "I, of course, mostly remember how wretched it was for Ruby Ferris and their young son."

Perhaps it was unfair of her to assume the solemn expression that immediately covered his face was false.

"Ah yes," he said. "Such a tragedy, for a young wife to lose her husband and a boy his father." He sighed gustily. "Your readers might be interested to know that I too was raised without a father, Miss Gray. Yet look how I succeeded! Young Ferris may very well thrive as I have, driven by a sorrowful childhood to make something good of his adult life."

This mill wasn't such a success, the nasty part of Pauline's mind said, but she restrained herself. She would not be petty! She couldn't help but ask, however,

"And what will you do when the mill shuts down, Mr. Wharton? I'm sure my readers will want to know."

"Ah." He blotted his face with the handkerchief again. "I could, of course, retire. I have enough put away safely to be able to live comfortably the rest of my days. But ..." Did he actually look embarrassed? "I don't know that I would ever feel right with my conscience, living well while my former employees were all struggling. I can't go into any details, my dear, but I can tell you I am looking into the possibility of opening a new business in the county, one which would hopefully give work to all the mill workers and more. I may lose the shirt off my back, but by gum, what a challenge!"

He jutted his head forward, showing her in a flash the real man who lived and breathed business under the surface geniality.

Pauline still couldn't like him, not least for that patronizing "my dear," but she was developing a reluctant respect for him.

"Perhaps in time you could take on and train Jeremy Ferris," she suggested.

His eyes brightened. "Now there's an idea! I'd like to do something for the lad and his mother. She wouldn't take any money from me at the time, you know. It wasn't charity, I wanted to show my respect and regret for Ferris, but I had to admire her stance." He paused. "It wasn't guilt, either. I accepted the fine because the mill was my responsibility, but that window was *safe*. I'd swear it."

"How do you think Bob fell, then?" she asked.

He shrugged. "A question I've asked myself many a time. If you ever get an answer, I'd like to hear it."

There it was—as close to proof that Bob was murdered as they were going to get. Pauline was no closer to finding the murderer, though she was inclined to write Mr. Wharton off after this conversation, but at least she was now certain they weren't chasing a will o'the wisp.

Wharton stood up. "And now, would you like a tour of the mill, Miss Gray?"

She agreed, thinking it would both be good in the article and might give her a hint as to how someone might have pushed Bob out the window without anyone else noticing, save mysteriously for Jemima Root.

She didn't understand much of the terms Wharton used as he extolled the superiority of their rollers versus conventional millstones, the ingenious way their elevator system worked, and the "middlings purifiers" that separated the dust, bran, middlings, and flour from each other, but she nodded and took notes while surreptitiously scanning the interior of the building.

Beneath the main floor was the old water turbine that had provided the energy for the mill until Wharton converted it to electricity. With all the grain elevators, pulley systems, and machines around, Pauline saw how easily a man could fall—or be pushed—from a third-floor window into the river without anyone noticing until too late. The dust floating in the air made it hard to make out details even on the floor she was on, much less the others.

"And this will interest you, Miss Gray," Wharton boomed, motioning to a stack of filled flour sacks waiting to be delivered. "We get our sacks specially printed with this pattern so that women can make frocks from it that look as fresh and pretty as anything in a big-city department store! I had thought of having a write-in competition, where people sent us designs and we chose our favorite to print on our next run, but ... alas. It doesn't seem likely there will be need to purchase any more. After the batch we have in stock is used up, we will be done."

Pauline found the large red poppies with vivid green leaves against a stark white background a little garish for her taste, but she made an admiring noise and jotted down a note. That was the sort of detail her female readers would appreciate.

"It's very bright," she said in what she hoped was an admiring voice, running her hand over one of the sacks that was set a little apart from the others.

Her fingers came away damp and sticky. She frowned, but before she could say anything about it to Wharton, he had moved on to something else. Pauline wiped her hand on her handkerchief and shrugged the incident off.

The tour ended, Wharton personally escorted her out the front door.

"Thank you for your time, Mr. Wharton," Pauline said.

"My dear, it was a pleasure! I look forward to reading your little piece in the *Times*. Who knows, perhaps it will attract investors when I embark on my new venture."

Tamping down irritation—her "little piece" indeed—

Pauline shook his hand and walked the short distance to where she'd left Jean-Paul's bicycle leaning against the stone wall lining the riverbank. As she rounded the corner, she was surprised to see an older woman standing next to it.

Pauline quickened her pace, wondering if there was a problem.

"Excuse me!" she called, just as the woman lifted her head and looked toward her.

"You there!" the woman called.

Pauline stopped. It took her a moment to recognize Iris Ferris in the gaunt, lined face of the lady before her. She had aged nearly twenty years in the four since her brother's passing.

"Oh," said Pauline, picking her way carefully down the leaf-strewn slope. "Hello, Miss Ferris."

Iris blinked a few times before recognition dawned on her own face. "Pauline Gray, the newspaper woman," she said, putting a wealth of scorn into her words.

Taken aback, Pauline forgot to be cautious and skidded forward on the slippery dead leaves, barely catching herself on a slim birch growing near the water's edge.

Iris laughed. "You want to be careful you don't bring about another accident here," she sneered. "Bash your head on the wall, or tumble right over it into the river. Can you swim, Miss Gray?"

Pauline regained her breath and her composure. She wondered if Miss Ferris was quite sane.

"As a matter of face, I can," she said.

She took the bicycle's handlebars and wheeled it toward the road. Iris trailed after her.

"Is that contraption yours?" she snapped.

Pauline considered her answer. Technically it wasn't, but she was the one responsible for it at the moment. "Yes," she said.

"It's a hazard," Iris said. "If someone were to injure themselves on account of it, you would be responsible, not the mill."

"What sort of injury could it cause, against the wall as it was?" Pauline inquired, eyebrows raised.

"Never mind," snapped Iris. "Bad things happen around this mill. You don't need to add to it."

Skepticism crept into Pauline's voice. "Bad things? You mean a curse?"

Iris's faded blue eyes flashed. "You can laugh, but you don't know! You weren't here the day my brother—when he—I was here! I know!"

Pauline had been wondering how quickly she could get away. Now she stopped.

"You were here the day your brother died?"

Iris's gaze slid away. "I was out for a walk," she mumbled. "No law against walking. I like the river."

Pauline steeled herself to rest a hand on Iris's arm in an appearance of sympathy. "Did you see your brother?" she asked, once again gentling her voice. "That must have been terrible."

"No—no!" the other woman cried, shaking free. "I saw nothing, but I felt it. I felt the evil here. There is a curse about this place! Jemima Root, she could have told you."

"What?" Despite herself, Pauline's voice rose sharply.

Iris nodded, seeming satisfied to have gotten a reaction at last. "You've heard about her death, then? I told you there was a curse. She was here that day, too. I didn't see her, but she saw him. She saw my brother fall! And now look what's happened to her."

"Jemima Root was killed by a human, not a curse," Pauline said. In a distant part of her mind, she noted her hands were shaking. This was the first proof they had to connect Miss Root to Bob's death.

Of course, if Iris Ferris was the murderer, Pauline was in terrible danger right now.

Iris stepped closer. "You think you're so smart, Ms. Newspaper Writer, looking down at the rest of us, wheeling around on your ridiculous bicycle without a care in the world. You're no better than I! You're just another spinster. One day you too will look around and realize you're all alone, with nobody to care if you live or die. You, me, Jemima ... we're all the same."

Pauline stepped backward. Were the stone walls too thick for anyone inside if she screamed? Would it do her any good to mention that people knew she was here?

"I'm afraid I really must be going now," she said inanely. "Goodbye, Miss Ferris."

With that, she hurled herself onto the bicycle with more force than elegance and pedaled away for dear life. She glanced back just once.

Iris Ferris was still standing beside the road, staring after her with a look of intense hatred on her face.

CHAPTER SEVEN

Panic and Peace

Still shaken by her encounter with Iris Ferris, Pauline couldn't face the idea of going back to an empty apartment for a lonely lunch. Pedaling into Canton, she stopped at the Sugar Bowl Restaurant to indulge in coffee and a bowl of soup. To her surprise, she met James at the counter.

"I think we should raise Iris Ferris to the top of our suspect list," she said without preamble.

"What? Why?"

"I was at the mill this morning—" she began.

His face turned an alarming shade of red. "Pauline, you promised!"

She steered him to a booth to sit before he choked. "I went

out there to interview Mr. Wharton for the paper, that's all," she said, a touch more defiantly than she intended. "All this talk about the mill closing and people being out of work made me realize that attention needs to be drawn to our local businesses, to support and promote them. Since the grist mill was so prominent in my mind, I pursued that one first." She made a point of glancing around the bustling restaurant interior. "I'm thinking of making this my next article."

James raised an eyebrow. "Really."

Pauline folded her hands and rested them on the table top. "Yes."

"And the reason you told me this in such detail is ...?"

"I don't want you to misjudge me," she said primly.

"If your conscience was absolutely clear on the matter, you wouldn't care what I or anyone else thought," he said.

She refused to let herself blush. "At any rate, I didn't bring up Bob, but Mr. Wharton did, and I don't think he was the one behind the death."

"Does he have an alibi?"

"Not that I could ascertain," Pauline said. "I didn't want to ask outright."

"Thank goodness for that," James said.

He broke off to accept his coffee and wrapped sandwich from Suzy, the petite red-headed waitress.

"Your soup will be right out, honey," Suzy told Pauline while setting a mug in front of her.

"Soup and coffee? It's not that cold," James commented.

Pauline shivered. "You wouldn't say that if you'd seen Iris Ferris."

At his urging, she told him the entire story. By the end, he still seemed skeptical.

"So she's crazy. It's well known that spinsters ..." He faltered at Pauline's steely glare, and coughed. "It doesn't prove anything. It doesn't even absolutely prove that Jemima Root's death is connected with Bob's."

"But Miss Ferris said Miss Root saw Bob die!"

"She also said the mill was cursed and your bicycle was going to kill someone," he said dryly.

He had a point.

"I agree that *if* Jemima Root saw something that could identify Bob's murderer, that person had a good reason to silence her. But why now, instead of four years ago? And why would she be quiet all this time and only now start writing to Ruby?"

"Guilt," Pauline suggested. "If it was Iris, then Miss Root wouldn't want to turn her in because they were friends. But she couldn't keep quiet forever, her conscience kept nagging at her, and she had to write to Ruby about it. Then she felt guilty about betraying her friend, confessed to Iris and Iris killed her." She leaned back. "And if you tell me I should be writing dramatic fiction, I shall throw this cup of coffee at your head."

He laughed. "Sorry. I suppose that sort of comment is galling to a serious writer like yourself, isn't it?"

Ouch. That one stung.

"You make it sound plausible, but the most reasonable explanation is still that some tramp broke into Miss Root's house to look for food and money, lost his head and killed her before escaping, and is probably heading for Canada right now. The letters are most likely coincidence." He shrugged. "That's the chief's theory, and he's probably right. There's a reason he's the chief and I'm a lowly lieutenant."

"For all you talk about me sounding like a blood-and-thunder writer, I know one thing," Pauline snapped. "I don't believe in coincidences except as convenient plot devices!"

He smiled good-humoredly at her, drained his coffee, tucked

his still-wrapped sandwich into his coat pocket, and left her to her cooling soup and temper.

Silly to get so irritated by his comment. She *was* a serious writer, after all. Not the novels, nor even the features. Oh, but she had dreams. More than dreams, she had plans!

Once she had enough savings built up in her bank account, she could take a break from her adventure novels and start serious research into a biography. Or a history. Or—well, she hadn't quite settled on it yet. She didn't have anything close to a thesis in place. But she knew it was there, the real work, waiting for her.

The newspaper column and novels were merely a way of getting by. Everyone had to start somewhere. They were good practice for when she was ready to get down to her real work.

A mocking voice in the back of her mind told her these were all very fine excuses, but who was she arguing against, James or herself?

Pauline finished her meal and left the restaurant in a distinctly sour mood. The laughing, chattering, bright-eyed college students filling the building and spilling over onto the sidewalk didn't help improve it. Soon enough, she thought darkly as she wound her way through the crowd, soon enough they'd graduate and face real life, and then they'd know.

What, exactly, they'd know, she couldn't say, but it would be something along the lines of how life never worked out the way you expected it to, and all those other clichés she had thought so foolish when she was eighteen.

She tripped and almost fell flat on her face when she reached the sidewalk and saw Jean-Paul's bicycle. Both its tires had been slashed, and somebody had dumped a bucket of black paint over the seat and frame, leaving the bucket dangling defiantly from the handlebars. It had to have been recently done—as she recovered and approached it to prod gingerly at the mess, her finger came away coated in wet black paint.

How was she going to explain this to Jean-Paul, was her first thought. How someone had done this in the middle of town without anyone noticing was her second. Her third, most chilling, was: someone wanted to scare her.

James's warnings to her came back in full force. They made more sense now.

"I told you the mill was cursed."

Pauline looked over sharply. Iris Ferris stood beside her, eyes glinting in satisfaction as she looked at the ruin of Jean-Paul's bicycle.

Fear vanished in a burst of sickening anger.

"You—you did this!" Pauline cried.

Miss Ferris did not deny it. "And if I did, what more do you think I might do to you?" she said, her voice soft and slippery.

Pauline's anger ebbed, leaving behind nausea and a terror that precluded rational thought. Iris Ferris was mad— unquestionably so—she had most likely murdered two people and had destroyed Jean-Paul's bicycle in the middle of town during the busiest part of the day. What was to stop her from trying to hurt or even kill Pauline herself?

As if in answer to her thoughts, the wind picked up, pushing clouds over the face of the sun to darken the day. Dry leaves whirled around Pauline's feet, rustling past and catching at her stockings with their rough edges. The crowds on Main had vanished, everyone inside a building where it was warm and light and safe. Across the street a lone black dog tied in front of the drugstore howled for its master.

Pauline took one, two, three steps back from the bicycle and the madwoman beside it. Where was James when she needed him?

Iris Ferris laughed.

Pauline's nerve broke, and she ran.

Had she kept her head even a little, she could have gone around the corner and run the back way to the little apartment on Pleasant St. Instead, she found herself crossing the road, narrowly missing being run over by a large green car driven by a portly man who shook his fist out the window and shouted something about "fool women" after her.

Past the library, so often a place of sanctuary but not a haven today, not when Iris Ferris could follow her in there. Past the houses lining the street and the side roads that would lead to secluded areas where anything—absolutely anything—could happen.

Pauline did not look behind her. She didn't want to know if Iris Ferris was following. She didn't want to know if her fears had any base in reality. She wasn't running away from Iris, not really. She was running away from the ugliness of the attack on the bicycle, from the violence that had erupted into her peaceful world, from her own horror and terror.

Of their own accord, her feet turned onto the long drive leading into the heart of St. Lawrence University. Under the overarching boughs of the trees lining the drive, with students and professors crossing the leaf-covered lawns, arms full of books and papers, chatting about their classes and interests, her heart slowed to a normal beat, and her feet slowed likewise.

When all other havens were lost, this one remained.

Pauline felt thoroughly ashamed of her panic. How could she have lost her self-control like that? She, who prided herself on her rationality, who shied away from strong emotions as messy and vaguely distasteful, to throw her poise and her calm detachment out the window without even a good reason.

Yes, it was horrid to have Jean-Paul's bicycle vandalized like that. Yes, Iris Ferris had shown alarming behavior. Yes, news of a murderer loose in Canton had people on edge. It was no excuse for giving way like that.

Pauline found her steps had led her to Gunnison Chapel, the Gothic-styled limestone building that served as the center of worship for St. Lawrence students. She hadn't spent much time there as a student, but it was familiar enough.

She slipped through the heavy front doors into the empty nave. Sitting in a back pew, she tilted her head back to look up at the vaulted ceiling, buttressed by old ships' timbers from Maine.

Pauline wasn't much for organized religion. She attended the Episcopal Church regularly, but she found the emotionalism of devout worship uncomfortable. All the same, she released the last of her fears and tension in a long breath as the quiet peace of the place seeped into her spirit.

Glancing down at her ungloved hands, she frowned at the black paint still marring her right forefinger. She pulled out her handkerchief to scrub at the stain and became aware of a strong odor of spirits filling the air.

Pauline sniffed, looking around. There was nothing in the building to cause that odor, not even communion wine. She looked at the handkerchief and brought it closer to her nose.

Ugh. No question but that was it.

Why should her handkerchief smell like a distillery?

Mind flashing back to the morning, Pauline remembered her hand brushing something wet and sticky on a flour sack, and using her handkerchief to wipe it off. The bag must have been soaked in alcohol. The flour inside would be ruined—

Her brain caught up with a jerk. Flour? No! It was alcohol that must have been inside that bag, bottles of Canadian whiskey smuggled across the river and hidden inside an innocuous, brightly-patterned sack to be sent on to New York City. One bottle must have broken and its contents leaked through.

Entirely by accident, Pauline had stumbled upon the smuggling ring at the mill.

But who was behind it? Andrew Wharton, the owner? Mr. Kitteredge, the foreman? Surely not Dan Harwood, or he wouldn't be so distressed over the potential loss of his job. Or— would he? With the mill closing, the smugglers would have to find a new way to hide their illicit goods for transport.

Or was it someone else entirely?

And where did Bob Ferris and his sister fit into all this?

It was with a newly calmed heart but a head full of new questions that Pauline rose and at last left the chapel. As she walked down the path leading off campus back toward town, the bells in the copper tower rang out their 5:00 peal.

It was time to go home.

The journey back to Pleasant St. seemed longer than usual. Pauline was tired and wrung-out after her emotional experience earlier. Her thoughts dwelled longingly on home, a cozy fire in the living room, conversation with Sarah, a simple meal.

Therefore it was with an unpleasant shock jolting through her body that she saw Iris Ferris waiting for her on her very doorstep.

"Miss Gray," the woman said. There was no trace of madness about her now. "I need to speak with you."

Pauline glanced up. Shining through the curtains of the second-story window was lamplight. Sarah was home. Even if Miss Ferris wanted to harm her, she could not prevail against the two of them.

"In that case," Pauline said, "you'd better come in."

CHAPTER EIGHT

Iris Ferris

Iris Ferris's first words, once inside and ensconced in the armchair James had sat in the previous night, were unexpected.

"I wish to apologize for my behavior this morning, and again this afternoon. I realized after you left so precipitously that I must have given the impression I meant you ill. I assure you, I had nothing to do with the damage to your bicycle, and I am sorry for the ... wild manner in which I spoke. I was not entirely myself."

Pauline's suspicions deepened. Was this a woman trying to cover her tracks? Who else could have damaged the bicycle, if not Miss Ferris? Who else knew Pauline was riding it?

Sarah interrupted. "Miss Ferris, please don't think me rude

if I ask when the last time was you ate."

The older woman hesitated. "Why—last night, I suppose. Sometime yesterday, at any rate."

"That will never do! No wonder you say you were not yourself. Wait right here. Pauline, I insist, no more questions or conversations until Miss Ferris has some food in her."

"No, really, I often skip meals," Iris protested, but to no avail.

"All the more reason to eat now," Sarah overrode her. "That is an unhealthy habit, if you will allow me to be blunt."

Miss Ferris sank back into her chair, and Pauline shrugged, offered a small smile, and built the fire while Sarah whisked out to the kitchen. Pauline ought to have gone with her—she didn't want to make Sarah wait on her guest—but neither did she feel comfortable leaving Miss Ferris alone.

"Chicken broth and a slice of white bread for now. Nothing too heavy until we see how this sits on the stomach," Sarah said, coming back in a few minutes with a tray holding a bowl of steaming bouillon, a place with buttered bread, and a tall glass of milk.

She set it on the small table beside the armchair and stood over Iris Ferris until the woman had consumed at least half of everything on the tray. Then, and only then, did Sarah agree to sit down and allow the conversation to proceed.

"I found out about Jemima Root this morning when I met the milkman on the front steps of Mrs. Griffith's," naming the owner of the boarding house where she lived. "I was shaken."

"Did you know her well?" Pauline asked, cautiously sympathetic.

Iris drank the last of her milk before answering. She set the glass down and stared into the flames flickering in the fireplace. "Jemima Root was the closest thing I have to a friend in this town," she said. "She had gotten odd these last few years, but so have I. We were schoolgirls together, she a few years ahead of I, but we were still close. We both dreamed of going past grade school, but our families couldn't afford university for either of us and felt high school was a waste of time. No man wanted to marry either of us: we were too sharp-tongued, too independent, not pretty enough. So we grew into spinsterhood together, cheated of our dreams and our families' hopes alike."

Pauline couldn't hold back a flinch. Were it not for her grandfather's emotional and financial support of her education before his death, she could be well on her way to a similar fate.

"When I heard she was dead—not only dead, but murdered, it shook me. I couldn't face going back in to breakfast with Mrs. Griffith's prying questions and the nosiness of my fellow boarders." Iris's lip curled in disgust.

"I went for a walk and found myself at my sister-in-law's house—what used to be mine."

Despite herself, Pauline leaned forward, her whole being caught up in the story. She tried to hold back, reminding herself that Iris Ferris was still her strongest suspect for the murder, but she couldn't help but believe the older woman's tale as it unfolded. If it was fiction, it was woven better than anything Pauline could write.

"The older I get the harder it is to hold onto hate," Miss Ferris said. "With the loss of my only friend, I wanted to reconcile with what family I had left." Her face worked against some strong emotion.

Without a word, Sarah rose and took the bowl back into the kitchen for more broth. Returning, she set it before Iris and settled back into her chair, nodding for the other to continue.

"Ruby wouldn't have anything to do with me. I knew she disliked me, but I'd never thought her spiteful! She wouldn't even unlock the door. Told me to go away through the keyhole."

"Ah," said Pauline, wondering how much to reveal.

"I left and kept walking, eventually finding myself at the mill —that wretched place which took my brother's life. Jemima saw him fall, though she would never tell me more about it than that, saying it was too distressing. Her death brought back the memories of his, on top of Ruby shutting me out of her and Jeremy's lives, and then I saw you—" She drew in a long, shaken breath.

"I think I understand," Pauline said.

But Iris wasn't finished.

"I don't remember much about my walk back to town, except that I saw your bicycle with its tires ruined and the black paint, and somehow it seemed to me a fitting punishment for ... something." She raised a thin hand and let it fall again. "I don't know now why I felt you deserved punishment, but I did. I didn't wreck your cycle, though, Miss Gray, and I'm only sorry I didn't see who did."

Sarah let out a brief exclamation. "Your bicycle? Pauline, what happened?"

Pauline explained, her mind working furiously. Iris's tale made sense. If it was true, she was neither the murderer nor the one who ruined Jean-Paul's bicycle—which, she reminded herself, she needed to fetch and have fixed before giving it back to him. Pauline had already ruled out Andrew Wharton.

That left John Kitteredge or an unknown mill worker and smuggler for the suspect list.

Before she could rule Iris out entirely, she would make one more test.

"Did you know that Jemima Root had been writing to your sister-in-law to say that Bob was murdered?"

Iris Ferris dropped her soup bowl onto the floor, where it

shattered into a thousand pieces, leaving shards of white porcelain in a pool of golden broth. Face white as paper, she slumped to one side in the chair, eyes fluttering back in her head.

Pauline sprang to her feet with no idea of what to do next.

"Really, Pauline!" Sarah exclaimed, a wealth of exasperation in her voice.

"Did I kill her?" Pauline asked, barely restraining herself from wringing her hands.

"Nonsense," Sarah said. "She's fainted. You clean up the mess, I'll bring her to."

Pauline meekly retreated to the kitchen for rags and the brush and dustpan.

Within a short time, Sarah had restored Iris to consciousness and Pauline had cleaned up the broken bowl and spilled soup. Following directions, Pauline made a cup of tea heavily laced with sugar and brought it for Iris to sip. Only once some color had come back to her cheeks did Sarah allow Pauline to apologize.

"I am so sorry, Miss Ferris," she said quietly, ashamed of suspecting her of murder as well as for the shock she had given the older woman. "I should never have said that."

"Is it true? Jemima believed my brother was murdered?"

Pauline rubbed her thumb nervously against the side of her forefinger. What to say?

"Tell her," Sarah said, holding Iris's wrist to check her pulse. "She'll only fret more unless you do."

"The letters were anonymous, but the police discovered that she was the author after—after her death."

"Why wouldn't she tell me? She must have seen it happen! Why haven't the police arrested anyone for his death? Is that why Ruby wouldn't let me in?"

"You believe her?" Sarah asked.

Iris seemed fully restored to life now. She waved an impatient hand. "Of course, Miss Jones. Jemima Root was not given to fancies. She was there that day. She must have seen it and been too afraid to tell anyone. Perhaps the killer threatened her."

That hadn't occurred to Pauline.

"But eventually she must have been no longer able to keep silent, so she did the only thing she could think of." She hit her open palm with her other fist. "Oh, if only she had come to me about it! She might still be alive."

"Or you could be dead, too," Sarah said cynically.

She must no longer have been worried about her patient's condition for that sort of comment to slip out.

Iris raised her chin haughtily. "I only wish the murderer had come for me, Miss Jones. I would have made him wish he'd never been born."

Pauline could well believe it.

"I think Ruby kept the door locked on you out of fear," she said now, turning the subject. "Lieutenant Richardson knows about the entire matter, and I believe he warned Ruby against letting anyone into the house until the murderer has been caught."

Iris sniffed. "Even her sister-in-law?"

There was an awkward silence.

"Ah. I see. I have been a suspect as well. Against my own brother? And my closest friend? No, no, I understand. Embittered by his marriage, I killed my brother, and of course a woman like me couldn't have a true friend." She broke into a rusty laugh. "No wonder you ran away from me earlier! Tell me, Miss Gray, am I still a suspect?"

Iris rose to her feet, her eyes flashing. Pauline stood as well. Though Iris was taller, Pauline carried herself with a natural dignity that bore up well against the other's height and indignation.

"I cannot speak for the police, Miss Ferris, but for myself, I no longer suspect you of any wrongdoing whatsoever."

"Neither do I," Sarah added.

Iris's shoulders slumped a little. "Thank you," she said. She sighed a little. "And to think I simply came here to assure you I had no idea how your bicycle was vandalized."

"I still don't understand how a thing like that could happen in the middle of the day on Main St," Sarah said, shaking her head.

"Quick enough work to stab tires with a penknife and overturn a bucket of paint before walking on," Pauline said. "I just want to know why. It isn't as though I've learned anything helpful. No one should feel the need to threaten me."

"Perhaps you saw or heard something that seems irrelevant to you, but to the murderer it seems of great importance," Sarah said. She frowned. "Oh, that's all muddled up. You know what I mean."

"Yes, I think I do," Pauline said. She thought again of the whiskey-saturated flour sack. Had someone noticed her drying her hand after touching it? Was the bicycle a warning to leave well enough alone?

She would tell Sarah about the incident after Iris left. Even with her new trust in Bob's sister's innocence, she wasn't ready to share everything yet.

"You could always ask John Kitteredge if he saw anything," Iris said. "I noticed him standing nearby as I came up to the restaurant."

John Kitteredge? But he hadn't even been at the mill that morning. He couldn't have seen anything to raise his suspicions, even if he was a smuggler or (or possibly and) a murderer.

Pauline pushed her hair back from her face. "I can't think about it anymore," she said, her voice trembling with exhaustion. "It's been a long day."

"And I am taking up too much of your evening," Iris said at once. "I'll leave you two now. Keep me informed about any progress with the case."

The light in her eyes showed it was a demand rather than a request.

It wasn't until after Pauline was in bed and drifting off to sleep that the most obvious question of all came to her:

Why had Jemima Root been at the mill the day of Bob's death?

CHAPTER NINE

At the Train Station

"You're up early." Sarah glanced up from the morning paper as Pauline stumbled into their tiny mint-green kitchen, heading straight for the coffee tin.

"Dreams," Pauline said briefly.

She plugged in the stainless steel percolator and spooned in the coffee. While she waited for it to brew, she stared out the small window above the sink, mind playing back over the dreams of running in the dark, chased by faceless men and women, people who both needed her help and meant her harm.

It had not been a restful night.

"Are you going to tell Lieutenant Richardson about the whiskey today?" Sarah asked, rising from the table to rinse her sticky oatmeal bowl.

Pauline sighed. She took a bowl of her own down from the cupboard and spooned oatmeal from the pot into it. Sitting down, she swirled maple syrup into the bowl, tracking the swirls and loops the amber liquid made over the oats. "I haven't decided."

Sarah turned from the sink, hands on her hips. "Haven't decided? What is there to decide?"

"The police seem more interested in stopping this smuggling ring than they do in solving the murders," Pauline said. "James is the only one who really cares. All the rest look at Miss Root as nothing but a lonely old spinster given to writing crazed anonymous letters, most likely murdered by a passing tramp, not much of a loss to anyone. If I tell James about the whiskey, it will take his attention away from the murders as well, leaving no one who will care enough to get to the heart of the matter."

"But if the smugglers are the ones who committed the murders, telling the police will solve both cases at once. Besides, it's your duty. Who are you to decide what information the police should have and which they shouldn't?"

Pauline pushed the oatmeal away, stomach twisting. She got up and poured herself a cup of the now-bubbling coffee, hoping that would settle her enough to be able to eat her breakfast. "What's the good of having a brain and a conscience if I don't use them? Deciding what information the police need and what will only get in the way is part of the responsibility I took on when I involved myself in this matter."

"That sounds dangerously close to arrogance," Sarah said bluntly.

"Anything else seems like cowardice to me," Pauline responded.

"Is it cowardice to recognize that someone vandalized your bicycle as an attempt to frighten you? That alone should tell you these people are dangerous. Even if it they don't have anything to do with the murders, you need to turn them in for the community's sake."

"And if turning them in means the case is closed on Jemima Root and never even opened for Bob Ferris? Is my own safety really worth that?"

Sarah shook her head. "I have to run or I'll be late to work. Think about it some more, please? You're not God; it's not up to you to make all things right. Sometimes you have to humble yourself enough to know you can't see everything, and to accept your limitations."

Her words rang in Pauline's ears even after she left.

Was she being arrogant in her hesitation? Was she abrogating too much authority onto her shoulders? It did seem as though deciding what information to share and what to withhold was a foolish action.

And yet ... she couldn't shake the thought that blindly handing everything over to James without sifting through it first was the act of someone who wanted the thrill of the chase without the burden of responsibility.

Though her stomach was still in knots, she forced herself to eat her breakfast so that it would not go to waste. As she scrubbed out the oatmeal pot afterward, she made her decision.

She would tell James—but she would gather more information herself first.

The first step would be recovering Jean-Paul's bicycle and finding John Kitteredge to ask if he saw anything. If he was the guilty party, Pauline could be putting herself in danger, but she couldn't see any way around it.

Whether it was arrogance or not, she couldn't walk away

from this now.

She finished the dishes and left to go back into town to fetch Jean-Paul's bicycle from its spot in front of the Sugar Bowl. There, she found a younger police officer looking at the bicycle and writing down some notes.

"Oh!" Pauline said, coming to a halt. "Good morning."

"Is this your machine, miss?" the officer said, looking over at her with an expression that strove for severity.

"No—yes—that is, I was using it when this happened, but it doesn't belong to me. I borrowed it from a friend."

"Ah," said the officer, making a note. "Then you were aware of this occurrence and yet you didn't report it or take care of it?" When Pauline hesitated, unsure of the best way to answer, he continued.

"Leaving a bicycle in this condition out in the street like this makes the entire town look bad, miss. It's a violation of propriety, that's what it is. It's an offense to people's eyes. It's—"

"I was going to report it today," Pauline interrupted, feeling a pang at this statement. She *would* have ... probably. Once she was certain it was her duty. And once she was certain it wouldn't make James order her off the case entirely. "I was too upset by it yesterday, when it happened."

A fatuous smile appeared on the officer's face. "Ah. Ladies' sensibilities. I understand, miss."

Pauline wanted to smack the smile off his face, but at the moment his assumptions were working in her favor, so she restrained herself.

"Any idea who might have done it?" the officer asked.

"Naturally not," Pauline said.

"Hmm ... your friend the owner, miss, would she happen to be a student?"

"He, and yes, he is."

The officer snapped his notepad closed and tucked it back into his pocket. "Ah-ha. As I suspected. A student prank. It's a distinctive contraption, and a fellow student most likely saw it and, not realizing you were using it, decided to play a trick on this student. Happens all the time."

Pauline found this theory highly unlikely. However, if it meant she could put off talking to James until after she'd spoken with John Kitteredge, so much the better.

"What we'll do now, miss, is I'll take the bicycle back to the station with me and we'll contact the owner and let him know what happened. If you'll give me his name?"

"Yes, of course. Jean-Paul Allain, at St. Lawrence University. And do let him know that I will of course pay for repairs if you cannot find the individual responsible for the damage, since the bicycle was in my care when it happened."

"Very kind and proper of you, miss, to be sure. Miss, ah ...?"

"Gray. Pauline Gray."

Enlightenment spread across the officer's face. "That's right, the newspaper lady! Using it in pursuit of a story?"

"Something like that."

He grinned at her. "Now, I don't suppose it would be a disgruntled interview-ee, upset about an article, would it?"

Pauline forced a laugh that sounded weak to her own ears. "Ahahaha. No. I doubt it."

The officer chuckled, tipped his hat, and wheeled the bicycle away.

"Next time don't wait to inform the authorities, Miss Gray!" he called over his shoulder.

Coming on the heels of her disagreement with Sarah as it did, it sounded like an ominous prophecy.

Pauline closed her eyes briefly before proceeding down the street, her heels clicking on the sidewalk with determination.

She had to do this her way. Though the whole world might stand against her, though in the end she might prove to be an utter fool for disregarding everyone's advice, even if it was hubris propelling her forward, her path was set.

She noted with absent surprise that her stomach had not twisted itself into knots and her throat hadn't closed from rising, formless panic. Either her attack of nerves yesterday had drained her enough that she didn't have the energy to be anxious today, or her determination to pursue justice on her own terms had steadied her for the first time since she got involved in this case.

She preferred to think it the latter.

It occurred to her as she walked that she didn't know exactly where she was going. Was John Kitteredge at the mill today? If so, how would she get there? How would she justify her return there to Mr. Wharton?

If she were exceptionally lucky, today would be the day Kitteredge was either delivering goods or picking up supplies from the train station and she could accost him there—but as she'd told James, she didn't believe in coincidences except as sloppy writing techniques.

Still, it did no harm to walk in the direction of the station and see. The station manager would know when people from the mill were supposed to be there for deliveries and the like. It was better than aimlessly wandering around town hoping for something to happen.

To the train station she accordingly went, nodding greetings at the people she passed, occasionally stopping to exchange courtesies. She smiled warmly at the small boy and only slightly-larger girl, brother and sister by their similar ears and chins, staggering out of the public library with arms full of books, arguing shrilly over who was going to read the new Doctor Dolittle book first.

It was another glorious September day, with the sun shining down warmly in a brilliantly cerulean sky and a crisp breeze swirling the leaves in people's lawns. Pauline spotted many people out raking, laughing and exchanging jokes with their neighbors, and more than once caught a heavenly whiff of fresh bread or apple pie baking through someone's open kitchen window.

Even though the country was in a Depression and a murder had happened in their own village, the people of Canton were resilient as always, refusing to let their troubles weigh them down and spoil their enjoyment of life. It was one of the things Pauline loved about living here.

"Oh yes, John will be here within the hour," the station master said when she reached the small brick building that served the town's train needs. "Yesterday was the day he came to pick up supplies, today is the day he drops off the flour to go down to Albany and New York City and them other big cities."

Pauline wondered why Dan Harwood had been at the station two days ago, then, if today and yesterday were the regular days for the mill's freight. A special order, must be. Or else something to do with the smugglers? Was she led astray by his apparent lack of wealth? Perhaps he was more upset about the mill's closure because it would curtail the smuggling operation than he was about being out of regular work.

Maybe Kitteredge was a red herring, only distracting her from what she needed to see.

She couldn't know for sure without talking to the man. She told the station master she was there to get further information on her piece for the *Times*, and he nodded and pointed her to a low wooden bench she could sit on to wait.

"Or you could—but no, I don't suppose that would be appropriate."

"What's that?" she asked, ears pricked.

"Oh, it's just that Miss Root, the one who was murdered. Her house is only a five minute walk from here. I thought at first that you might want to take a look, you being a reporter and all, but I don't suppose that's the sort of story you cover, what with you being a lady."

Pauline's curiosity rose, and she stood with it. "As a matter of fact, I believe the editors of the paper would appreciate a report from someone on hand. Give it a personal touch," she added, seeing his horrified expression. "Talk about the woman's gardens or something. Show that she was a real person who should be mourned, not just another number, like in the cities."

His expression cleared. He plainly was still doubtful about the propriety of the matter, but was not as shocked and horrified as if she had set herself up as a hard-boiled reporter going after a sensational scoop.

"Right you are, miss. The house is that way," he said, pointing down a side street. "Little place, painted yellow, two apple trees in front. Can't miss it. I'll give you an interview, if you like," he added, puffing his chest out. "The police have already talked to me. Seems they think the murderer must have gotten away by the train, wanted to know if I could tell them who got on and off that morning. I told them no one! No trains stopped at all that morning, there was a problem further down the line and so everything was delayed until the afternoon. They weren't too pleased with that, I must say, but it wasn't my fault."

"Quite so," said Pauline, mostly to stem the flood of eloquence. She nodded her thanks to him and walked in the direction he'd indicated.

This in no way fit with her promise to James—this was active investigation with a vengeance—but she couldn't hold back now.

Besides, she felt in a way she owed it to the dead Jemima Root to learn a little more about her. If Pauline was going to take up the banner of justice on her behalf, it was only right she know something about the way she lived, the things she cared for, what went into making her the person she was.

To be a voice for the voiceless involved knowing who those people were as individuals, not just a silent mass.

CHAPTER TEN

Smugglers

Jemima Root had lived in a small yellow cottage with white trim and shutters and a tidy garden along the porch. As the station master had promised, two apple trees stood in front, one on either side of her closed front door, their boughs hanging low with ripe, unpicked fruit.

"Seems a shame to let them go to waste, doesn't it?" sighed a voice beside her. Pauline started and looked over.

A woman in a house dress and apron leaned on the fence between Miss Root's house and the house next door. She nodded at the trees.

"The apples, I mean. It would be disrespectful to pick them, I know, but it somehow seems worse to let them hang there until they rot. Poor Jemima. She was so proud of those trees. Called them her 'orchard' and gave away baskets of the apples to all her friends and neighbors."

Pauline swallowed. "She sounds like a lovely person."

The neighbor laughed. "She does, doesn't she? It's funny, though. She was as sharp-tongued and sour-faced as they come, and nobody thought much of her when she was alive. Only now we remember all the good things she did without anyone noticing, all the kind acts hidden behind her sharp words." She sniffed and dabbed her eyes with the apron edge. "It's actually not that funny, come to think of it."

Pauline stood awkwardly, unsure of what to say next. The neighbor saved her the trouble.

"Edna Wright. You're Miss Gray, the newspaper lady, aren't you?"

Once again Pauline marveled at how many people knew her by sight without her having any idea who they were in return. "Yes, that's right."

Ms. Wright scowled. "I wouldn't talk to most reporters, vultures they are, but you, well ... you're almost like one of us. You'll treat her respectfully, won't you?"

"I will," Pauline said, though she felt a pang of guilt at deceiving this woman.

Though she was not, in fact, writing a piece on Jemima Root, seeking her murderer was the most respectful thing Pauline could think of to do for her. It wasn't what this woman meant, but it would have to do.

"Were you here the day it happened?" she asked now. The police would have already questioned all the neighbors, of course, but it never hurt to ask again. There was a chance someone might have remembered something, or that they would speak more freely to Pauline than they would to a policeman.

The woman shook her head. "Oh no. I wish I was, I might have been able to help! I was visiting my sister who lives in Potsdam. She just had her sixth, and I promised I would stop by and help out, bring them some food ..." She trailed off. "Not that it matters. The point is I wasn't here. The first I learned of it was when I got home that evening and found the police here and everything all in an uproar." She shivered. "I made sure to lock our doors that night, you can believe me! Even if it was just a passing tramp, I won't take any chances."

"Indeed not," Pauline murmured.

Ms. Wright waved at the house on the other side of Miss Root's. "Now Betty there, she was home. She might be able to tell you something. She's not the one who found Jemima, though. That was Rick Tracy, across the road. He dropped by with some crab-apple jelly from his wife, walked into the kitchen and found her lying there on the floor, head bashed in." Her color changed and she swallowed hard.

Pauline felt queasy herself. James had carefully *not* given her any details of how Miss Root had been killed. She had, perhaps, been annoyed at his over-protectiveness, but now she found herself grateful he had spared her sensibilities. Even in her novels she tended to shy away from detailed descriptions of violence.

"How dreadful," she managed.

"Screamed like a small girl, he did," said Ms. Wright, regaining her composure and speaking with a hint of smugness.

"I will speak with both of them," said Pauline. "Thank you."

Betty, possessor of a dark red house tucked back among the oak trees and a taciturn disposition, could not or would not give Pauline any more information than the first neighbor did. She seemed to consider the entire affair vulgar, and Pauline a ghoul for showing interest in it. Mr. and Mrs. Tracy, across the road, were more forthcoming.

"Oh, it was dreadful," gasped Mrs. Tracy, bouncing her whimpering baby on her shoulder. "He's teething," she said in an aside, and then continued with the story. "Jemima has—had —always been kind to us, sending us food when this little one was born, teaching our eldest—Rachel, she's at school now—to read when the school teachers had all but given up on her, even bringing us chicken soup this summer when I fell ill. So when I made crab apple jelly last week, it seemed the least I could do to send a jar to her."

"Yes," said Pauline, hoping Mrs. Tracy would get to the point soon.

Whether she would have or no, her husband, a gaunt, grim man sitting in the corner of the kitchen took up the tale instead.

"And when I got there, she was dead. On the floor, head crushed, the poker from her own fireplace beside her, papers and ink scattered all over the kitchen table. I've never seen anything like it. Hope I never do again."

Papers and ink ... "As though she had been in the middle of writing something?"

Mr. Tracy nodded. "Yep."

"Jemima was very intelligent, Miss Gray," Mrs. Tracy hurried into speech again. "Always reading or writing something. Though lately she'd been more secretive about her writings ... she'd hide them under the newspaper or something like that whenever anyone stopped by. I assumed she was trying to write a book or the like and didn't want anyone to know." She sighed. "I guess we'll never know now. Her nephew, when he came to collect all her things, burned all her papers. I saw the bonfire in the backyard myself. Seems a shame, but maybe that's how Jemima wanted it."

Pauline barely heard this, her mind wrestling with the

question of why an intelligent woman, always reading and writing, one who could teach a child to read when the schoolmarm had given up on her, would have written such illegible letters.

Ah. To disguise her identity, of course. Poorly-spelled, grammatically incorrect letters would hide an educated woman's brain quite well, even a self-educated woman.

Pauline had a flash of insight into the dead woman: denied her chance at high school or college, starving for knowledge, doing her best to gain that knowledge on her own and use it for the good of others, enduring the reputation of oddity, frustrated in her dreams and nearly friendless but still striving to improve her life and the lives of her neighbors ... Pauline was pierced with sorrow that she'd never met Jemima Root and that now she'd never have the chance.

A murderer destroyed not only the person killed, but a part of all the people that individual had touched or might have touched. For someone like little Rachel Tracy, she lost a teacher and friend who might have helped her achieve the dreams Jemima Root had been denied. For Mrs. and Mrs. Tracy and the rest of the neighbors, it was a friend in need. For Iris Ferris, it was her only friend. And for Pauline, it was a woman who might have enriched her life greatly.

Pauline was more determined than ever to bring this murderer to justice, not only for the sake of the victims, but for the community who was so injured by this deed in ways many of them might never realize.

"Thank you for your time," she told the Tracys, checking her watch to see that it was nearly time for the train to come in. "I'm afraid I must be off."

"I'm glad to think there's someone out there who cares enough about ordinary people like Jemima—like us—to see to it her name isn't forgotten in some corner of the obituaries," Mrs. Tracy said.

Pauline experienced a moment of guilt over that—this was now the second time she had used her journalism as a cover to gain information without much intention of following through on a story, and the dishonesty of her actions combined with the trust of others ate away at her.

She vowed that as soon as she had finished this case, she *would* write up something about Jemima Root, a tribute to a woman overlooked in life and barely noticed in death, and she would insist her editor publish it.

For now, she must hurry back to the train station.

The station master met her return with a nod.

"You're just in time, miss. The train's come in and Kitteredge is here supervising the loading. Ho, John! Here's the lady wanting to see you I mentioned earlier."

A tall, broad-shouldered, square-jawed man looked over from where he was hoisting a bag of flour onto his shoulder from the wagon bed preparatory to placing it in the freight car.

To the best of Pauline's knowledge, she'd never seen him before. Yet upon setting eyes on her, John Kitteredge turned white, dropped the flour sack with a dull thud, and turned tail and fled.

The station master's jaw dropped. He pushed back his cap to scratch at his grizzled hair. "Well now ... what do you suppose that was about?"

Pauline ached to chase after Kitteredge, but she held herself back. For one, his legs were longer and he could easily outrun her. For another, if he were the murderer, as seemed increasingly likely, it would be extreme folly to present herself to him as another victim. Here in the train station, surrounded by witnesses, she was safe. On a quiet back street somewhere, not as much.

"Did you tell him who exactly it was looking for him?"

"No, just that someone had dropped by to see him and would be back before he left. Why?"

So his sudden panic was on recognizing her specifically. How did he know her by sight, when she could have passed him on the street without giving him a second look? Granted, more people knew who she was than she did them, as Edna Wright had proven earlier, but it still seemed odd.

And what did he have to fear from her, that her very presence should cause him to flee?

"Sir," Pauline said to the station master. "Do you have a telephone here?"

"Sure do," he answered, still staring after Kitteredge's vanishing figure. "But I can't let you use it. Station business only."

Pauline released a breath, aware that she had made her decision about the smuggling after all. This wasn't what she had wanted, but it was the only option left. Sarah would be pleased, at least. Pauline was not.

"I need you to call Lieutenant James Richardson of the Canton Police Department and tell him to come down here at once to receive evidence of smuggling."

The station master jerked his attention back to her. "Smuggling! On *my* trains?"

"I'm afraid so," Pauline said.

"Do you have proof?"

She nodded at the fallen flour sack, now discolored on one side from liquid seeping out of its contents. "There's your proof. Unless you know of another reason why flour would leak? There's whiskey in that sack, sir."

The station master swore, blushed and apologized, and

darted for the telephone.

Pauline, sick at heart and with aching feet, sat down on the wooden bench to await James's arrival.

CHAPTER ELEVEN

The Truth

It didn't take long to explain the situation to James and the bright young Officer Wallace accompanying him. They tore open the flour sacks as soon as they grasped the facts, revealing whiskey bottles nestled inside the soft flour in six of them.

"Well!" said James. "This settles it. Wallace, you get back to the station and tell the chief. We need to bring Kitteredge in for questioning, and we'll need a warrant to search the mill."

"D'you suppose Mr. Wharton is in on it too, Lieutenant?" Officer Wallace breathed, looking at the bottles with their amber contents in awe.

"That's one of the things we need to find out," James answered. He made a shooing motion with his hands, and the freckled, red-headed young policeman finally tore himself away to ride his bicycle back to the Town Hall to mobilize the forces.

"Well done, sir," James said to the station master. "You've answered the question that's been plaguing us for ages, how the smugglers were transporting the whiskey from the river to the cities. They must hide it in the grain to get it to the mill, and then in the sacks to transport it to the city. By gum, there must be an entire network of people involved! Now that we've uncovered the center of the web, though, the rest will fall into place."

The station master looked pleased, but wouldn't take another's praise. "Thank you, Lieutenant, but it's really Miss Gray here you have to thank. She was on Kitteredge's trail even before he got here, and she's the one who noticed the whiskey leaking after he ran away. It's a pity he knew you were on to him, Miss Gray, or we might have caught him in the act, but I'm sure these fine officers will catch him before long. He won't be leaving town on one of my trains, that's for certain."

James's eyes narrowed as Pauline assumed a demure expression. "Really. How providential, Miss Gray. Tell me, how did you suspect John Kitteredge of smuggling?"

"I never reveal my sources," Pauline said firmly.

James took her arm in a courteous yet unbreakable grip and hustled her to the end of the platform away from the station master and all the idle bystanders.

"Pauline, what on earth are you up to?"

"None of your business," she snapped, recognizing the illogic of the statement even as she spoke it. What was smuggling and murder if not James's business? And what would she know about any of this had he not involved her in it to begin with?

Her palms tingled and her breath shortened in her chest, a sure sign that her nerves were acting up again. Pauline concentrated on breathing in and out as slowly and steadily as she could, waiting for her racing heart to slow to normal before speaking again.

"I thought we had a deal," James said. "You promised you would stay out of active investigation. First you go out to the mill, now you come here to confront Kitteredge—how is any of this keeping quiet and safe?"

"The mill was for a story," Pauline said. "The rest of it ..." There were no more excuses. She would have to tell James all.

She told him how her hand had come away wet from a flour sack, and how only later had she recognized the smell as alcohol, and only after that had made the smuggling connection. Rather than tell of her struggle with her conscience over whether or not to tell him anything about the matter, she merely stated that she wanted further proof before talking to him about it, and thought it worth investigating if it had any connections to the murders on her own.

"And yes, I realize that I broke my promise to you in doing that," she said. "I am sorry."

"I should hope so," he said, anger still evident in the tight line of his mouth and hard light in his eyes.

"I've also realized that you were wrong in making such a request of me," she continued. "Or rather, not you, but that I was wrong in agreeing to it. When it comes to justice and truth-seeking, I cannot hide behind my sex or my profession. If there's something I can do, I must do it."

"Even if it puts you in danger?" James pressed.

"Even then," she said.

Her stomach stopped twisting. Apparently uncertainty, more than danger or distress, brought about her crises of nerves. Uncertainty about herself, uncertainty about the world, uncertainty about the right thing to do. Once there was something she could do, no matter how unpleasant, her strength returned.

Perhaps it wasn't living in the country at all that had saved her, but rather finding a community where she belonged, where she could give something of value and receive goodness from others in return. These murders had upset the balance, and if she could help restore it, she would.

Whatever it took.

James's face eased back into its more regular expression of good humor. "I'm not happy about it, but I suppose I can understand. I'm still going to nag at you to be careful, and to not do stupid things like put yourself deliberately in danger without telling anyone, just for a clue."

"Believe it or not, I appreciate that," she said. "And I will do my best to comply, particularly with that last point."

He laughed. "All right. Thank you for your help here. Are you going to be offended if I now ask you to go home and let us take care of things?"

"Do you think Kitteredge is the murderer as well as a smuggler?" she asked.

James sighed, his eyes drifting in the direction of Jemima Root's house. "I don't know. There's a good chance of it, but ... I suppose that's one of the things we'll have to ask him when we catch him. At this point, I don't even know if he's the head of the ring or merely a pawn."

Pauline thought back over her interview with Andrew Wharton. "For what it's worth, I doubt Mr. Wharton knows anything about it. I don't like the man, you understand, but he seems too shrewd a businessman, not to mention too proud of building the mill up by his own wits and hard work, to engage in something like smuggling."

"Your opinion means a lot to me. Whether the chief agrees is another matter," James said. "We'll see what turns up when we search the mill."

"And James—" Pauline didn't quite lower herself to grab him by the coat lapel, but he must have sensed her urgency for he stopped in the middle of stepping away and instead turned back to her.

"Yes?"

"You won't—don't let them use this as a distraction from Jemima Root and Bob. They deserve more than to be a footnote in a successful smuggling case."

He nodded once, soberly.

It was the best Pauline could do.

She left the station to make her way back home, mulling over the events of the morning. She couldn't help but feel there was something she'd missed, some small, personal detail she'd overlooked in the excitement of the larger picture. What was it?

The matter nagged at her the entire way back to the apartment, where she firmly set it aside in order to put in some solid work. She'd been neglecting her writing these last few days, too busy chasing after clues and criminals.

She had to write the story on the mill to send to her editor, along with a note that she intended to make this a series. She had to finish the edits on *Emma Daring: Danger in the Wild West* in order to get that in to her publishers in time. And she supposed she really ought to think about preparing supper for a change; it might be nice to have something other than soup out of a can with sliced bread on the side.

Pauline tossed her hat and coat on the side table and sat down at her desk, clearing her mind of all distractions for at least this space of time.

Some three hours later, she pushed her wooden chair back across the floorboards until its back feet caught as usual on the edge of the rag rug. With a sense of satisfaction, Pauline stood up and stretched her arms as high above her head as they could go, bending from one side to the other before reaching down to touch her toes. She repeated this a few times until she was able to fully disengage her brain from the distant place it went when she wrote and return it to the real world.

She neatly replaced the chair in front of the desk, put the cover back on the typewriter, straightened the rug and hung up her hat and coat, and sighed deeply.

This might not be the kind of scholarly work she had expected to do when she finished college, but it was satisfying in its own right. It had been rather clever, the trick she had used to allow Emma to rescue her niece and nephew—

Nephew.

That was it! That was the niggling detail she'd been trying to remember. Mrs. Tracy had said something about Miss Root's nephew coming and burning all her papers.

Who was he?

Supper would have to wait. Pauline was on the trail of another clue. It might prove a dead end, but she had to follow it through just in case.

Hat and coat back on, she exited the apartment and hurried down the steps, orienting herself in her mind to the location of Mrs. Griffith's boarding house. Iris Ferris was clearly the person to ask about Jemima Root's family.

The air had more of a chill than that morning. Pauline couldn't help a smile at the houses lining the streets, fancying them huddling together against the coming cold. Winter would be here soon enough. Boys and girls trick-or-treating on Halloween night in a month could be wearing snow boots and heavy coats over their costumes; it had happened before.

In the meantime, she enjoyed these days of it being cold

enough to wake one up, but warm enough to be able to step outside without ten extra layers. Many of the trees had shed their leaves, leaving bare branches to stretch against the sky and provide a contrast with the brilliant reds and golds still defiantly hanging on neighboring branches.

It was a scene to rejoice an artist's eye. Pauline had no skill with pen or pencil in that way, but perhaps Sarah would take advantage of the sunshine when she finished her shift at the hospital. They had one or two of her sketches hanging on their walls already; the young nurse had a talent for art that never ceased to amaze Pauline.

Mrs. Griffith was out doing the daily marketing when Pauline arrived at the boarding house, so she was able to meet Iris in the parlor without having to worry about anyone eavesdropping on their business.

"Miss Ferris, who was Miss Root's nephew?" she asked without preamble.

Iris didn't bat an eyelash at the abrupt question.

"Dan Harwood. His mother is—was—Jemima's younger sister."

Pauline stared at the ugly flowered wallpaper on the parlor walls as her mind began putting pieces together.

So that was why Miss Root had been at the mill the day of Bob's death. She was coming to visit her nephew.

Her nephew who was facing demotion or even losing his job while Bob Ferris was going to get a promotion.

Her nephew who got a raise once Bob was no longer there, who might have expected to get the promotion due to his seniority.

Her nephew who was in the village the day Jemima Root was killed.

Her nephew who had asked Pauline to not tell anyone she

94

had seen him that day, and who claimed to be picking up supplies at the station on a day no train stopped.

Her nephew whom Miss Root might very well have felt impelled to protect even if she saw him doing something dreadful.

Like murdering a man.

Pauline stopped herself, appalled.

Dan Harwood? No, no. Not someone she felt pity for, someone she almost liked. He had a mother and three siblings depending on him for their livelihood.

Why couldn't it be John Kitteredge, a man she'd never met, a man who most likely destroyed Jean-Paul's bicycle as a warning to her after one of his fellow smugglers at the mill warned him she'd seemed too interested in the flour sacks, a man whom the police were already after?

For a moment, Pauline was tempted to leave the matter, to walk away. Let the police charge Kitteredge with the murders as well as the smuggling. Let Dan go free.

Her entire being, soul and body alike, cringed away from that. How could she live, knowing she had hidden the truth? How could there be justice for the dead? Ruby and Jeremy deserved better—Iris deserved better—little Rachel Tracy and all those other lives touched in one way or another by the dead people deserved better.

Bob and Jemima themselves deserved better. Pauline couldn't give them back their lives, but she could give them truth. It was all she had.

She stood up.

"I need to see James."

"Right," said Iris Ferris, watching her with keen, if faded, blue eyes. "I'm coming with you."

CHAPTER TWELVE

At the Mill Again

Pauline managed to convince Iris to wait for her inside the Town Hall until Pauline had found James. As one who had been influential in uncovering the smuggling operation as well as a journalist, Pauline's interest in the case was easily explained. Iris Ferris, on the other hand, was an anomaly, and Pauline was afraid the officers wouldn't speak as freely in front of her.

She left Iris browsing through the paperback novels at the newsstand, noting with ironic amusement that the older woman had picked up the latest Emma Darling book and was leafing through that in an attempt to look busy.

Meanwhile, Pauline made her way to the police headquarters, tucked away in the back of the building. She was in luck—Officer Wallace was on duty at the front desk.

"Hello, Miss Gray!" he said, nearly bouncing up from his seat before settling down with an attempt at dignity. "That was some excitement this morning, wasn't it?"

"Yes, it was," Pauline agreed. "I need to see Lieutenant Richardson; is he in?"

"I'm afraid you just missed him; he left five minutes ago."

"I see," said Pauline. She wondered if she could persuade Wallace to tell her where James had gone. Probably not.

In the end, it wouldn't matter if she waited until this evening to tell James about Dan Harwood. A few more hours wouldn't hurt.

"I'll speak with him later, then," she said, starting to turn away.

"If you're here for more information about the smuggling operation, I can't tell you much, but I can tell you that Lieutenant Richardson is off making an arrest right now! And ..." Officer Wallace leaned over the wide mahogany desk, eyes glittering as he hissed, "We now believe the smuggling is connected to the murder of Jemima Root!"

That stopped Pauline in her tracks. "What?"

Officer Wallace sat back down. "Oh," he said, suddenly reticent. "I probably shouldn't have even said that much."

Pauline covered her emotions with a mask of polite interest. "Not to worry, I won't give any information to my editor until someone here has given me permission. Since you have told me this much, you can't leave me in suspense now. Who ... who is being arrested?"

"Well, you already know the warrant is out for Kitteredge's arrest. But it seems ... I shouldn't tell you this, but I guess it can't hurt ... it seems Andrew Wharton was behind the whole thing! Can you beat it?"

"What?" Pauline said, annoyed to hear her voice squeak. Really, she thought she had better self-control than this.

How had this happened? She had specifically told James she thought Wharton was innocent, and he'd—well no, he hadn't agreed, but he had at least listened and respected her opinion.

Or had he? Had he only been humoring her? She hated to think that of him.

"The chief told Lieutenant Richardson that since he was the one to crack the case, he could be the one to make the arrest. The lieutenant didn't even want to! He's a swell guy, but that's carrying modesty a little too far, if you ask me."

Now she understood. James was carrying out orders against his own judgement. This way, if there was a mistake, the chief could push the blame onto James's shoulders. He was a scapegoat.

She couldn't let that happen. She had to get out to the mill and stop James before it was too late.

"Thank you, Officer," she said to the young Wallace, and left before he could stop to think of asking why she'd come by in the first place.

At the newsstand, Iris dropped the book she was holding and rushed to meet her.

"Well?" the older woman demanded.

"I need to get to the mill," Pauline said. "I don't suppose you have an automobile?"

Iris sniffed. "Do I look like I inherited wealth from *my* grandparents?"

Pauline ignored this. Her grandparents hadn't been all that wealthy, but she had grown used to the assumption she was living off her family's money—how else could she afford to exist on her meager salary from the newspaper?

"James is about to arrest the wrong man, and I have to stop

him before it's too late," Pauline said.

Nobody had ever accused Iris Ferris of being dense. "Right," she said, taking the lead out of the building. "We need to find Mrs. Hansen."

"What—why?" Pauline didn't want to drag anyone else into this.

"She has a car which we can borrow. I'll drive; you explain as we go."

Pauline protested, but Iris ignored everything she said. Finally, Pauline capitulated. She'd always considered herself to have an iron will, but she looked positively flimsy compared to Iris Ferris.

To her surprise, the Episcopalian minister's wife did indeed let them take her car without any questions, requesting only that they fill the tank with gasoline before returning it.

In a shorter time than Pauline would have believed possible, they were whizzing along the road out of Canton toward the Wharton Grist Mill.

"Yes, she keeps the auto solely for the use of other people," Iris said in response to Pauline's bewilderment. "She says there's always somebody who needs to get someplace off the bus route, or too far for a bicycle, or who doesn't have a horse."

Pauline had to adjust her mental image of Mrs. Hansen as a woman who was kind-hearted but weak in the face of society's expectations to a person who did the best she could for other people within the bounds of her role. They couldn't all be zealots.

"Now, tell me!" Iris demanded.

Pauline wrenched her mind away from philosophical musings and explained the chain of events and her reasoning thereof that had led her to this place.

She barely finished when Iris pulled to a stop in front of the mill, right behind the black-and-white police car.

Pauline didn't hesitate. She wrenched open the door and leapt out. Most of the mill workers were gathered out front in small knots, muttering to each other and eyeing the doorway speculatively. Pauline approached the nearest.

"Where is Lieutenant Richardson?"

The man nodded at the door. "Inside with the boss. Why?"

Leaving Iris to answer, Pauline ran inside, heading for Andrew Wharton's inner office. She darted around the abandoned equipment and half-filled bags with single-minded purpose, oblivious to any distractions.

She did notice when an arm of steel encircled her neck, dragging her to a choking, sputtering stop.

"I knew you suspected me, but I thought I'd thrown you off my scent," panted Dan Harwood's voice in her ear. "I can't let you betray me now, not when I'm finally safe."

"Glugg," said Pauline, prying at his arm with her fingers.

It was no good. She was a relatively strong woman, but she couldn't loosen that rock-solid grip. A mill worker far outweighed a writer in strength and fitness.

She twisted and turned, trying to slip away, scrambling to stomp his feet, but she couldn't stop him from inexorably dragging her back, down the steps to the lowest level of the mill, down where the water glistened under the water turbine no longer in use.

"I don't want to kill you," he said, and sounded like he genuinely meant it.

He was going to, though. He would hit her over the head and throw her in the water, and she would drown just like Bob. Everyone would say, "Oh, another tragic accident," and Dan Harwood would get away with three murders.

He didn't know about Iris, though. He didn't know that

Pauline had already told everything to another person. Even if he killed her, he wouldn't be safe.

If only he would let her speak so she could tell him!

Pauline had a moment's hope that Iris might have seen Dan grab her, but as the moments passed and the other woman did not appear, that hope vanished. If they'd stayed on the main level there was a chance, but down here, no one could find them.

"I never wanted to kill anyone," Dan continued. Spots danced in front of Pauline's eyes as his grip tightened yet further.

He wouldn't knock her on the head, she realized. He would simply choke her until she lost consciousness and then let her slip into permanent oblivion in the dark waters beneath the mill.

"I needed that promotion Ferris was getting," he went on. "We needed that money! And then old Wharton went and gave it to Kitteredge instead. Serves him right, getting arrested for this murder. It is his fault, if he weren't so tight-fisted he wouldn't have driven me to that extreme. I didn't mean Bob to die! Just be out of commission for a little while, so I could take his place. It was sheer bad luck he hit his head on that rock.

"Then Aunt Jemima had to see it, and see me looking out the window after him. The old woman should have held her tongue—I was her nephew! Instead she went and wrote all those letters to Ruby, dragging it all up. It was only a matter of time before she told the police everything. I had to kill her when I stopped by that morning and saw the letter she was writing to Ruby. It was the only way!

"I knew, the moment you showed up at the mill, that you were on my trail. That's why I telephoned Kitteredge that you were onto his smuggling scheme. I figured he could scare you off, and even if you figured out he was the one who vandalized your bicycle, you'd pin the murder on him instead. After all, I'd known about the smuggling he'd been doing under Wharton's nose for years without splitting on him, and he never even offered me a cut. Why shouldn't he take the fall for me? It ought to have worked perfectly. Why'd you have to come back?"

Pauline couldn't speak—she couldn't breathe—she was going to die right there and her death wouldn't do anyone any good at all.

She was a moment from despair when there was a resounding *CLANGGGGGGG* from behind her and Dan Harwood's arm fell away.

Pauline fell forward on her hands and knees, retching and gasping for air. She barely heard the startled shouts from above, nor took any notice of James and another officer thundering down the steps to come to her aid.

Seared into her brain, even in the dim, uncertain light, was the image of Iris Ferris standing over Dan Harwood's prone body, a corrugated metal roller from an old separator held high in her hand, looking for all the world like a Valkyrie of the north.

"Never mind about Andrew Wharton," she said in a ringing voice. "This is the man who killed my brother and Jemima Root, and who tried to kill Miss Gray as well. I heard his entire confession."

James knelt down beside Pauline, checking her neck for damage. "What did I tell you about not rushing stupidly into danger?"

She managed a weak smile. "At least I brought Miss Ferris with me."

It was all rather anticlimactic after that. James and the other officer released Wharton, cleared now of both the murder charge and the smuggling charge thanks to Dan's statement. They arrested Dan once he came around. He didn't even try to deny the charges, instead continuing to blame his actions on everyone but himself.

His most vitriolic hate was directed toward Pauline.

After he was dragged into the police car and taken back to town, Iris helped Pauline into Mrs. Hansen's automobile.

"Shall I take you to the hospital?" she asked, looking at Pauline.

Already bruises were darkening around Pauline's throat.

"No," Pauline croaked. "Sarah will be back by now. I just want to go home."

"Very well." Iris cleared her throat as she pressed the starter. "I suppose I should apologize. I saw that man lurking in wait for you, and I dropped back so as to catch him in the act. I ought to have come to your rescue at once, but it occurred to me that if I could hear him confess, it would make the case much stronger against him than your train of logic. I didn't anticipate him harming you quite so much."

"It will pass," Pauline said. "I'm only thankful you were there at all. You saved my life."

Iris was still unsmiling, but Pauline detected a treacherous shimmer in her eyes as she answered.

"You deduced who killed my brother and my friend. Even though it didn't affect your life. Even though you didn't have to. Your life wouldn't have needed saving if you hadn't pursued the truth so vehemently. Thank you."

"You're welcome," Pauline said awkwardly.

It wouldn't bring back the dead. It wouldn't magically heal the hurt done to those left behind. Ruby and Iris would still need to come to terms with their relationship. Jeremy was still going to have to grow up without a father. The community would feel the gap left behind by Jemima's death.

But hopefully, with truth revealed and justice done, they could all begin to heal in a way they couldn't before, and their path forward would be made a little easier.

Despite her bruises and the shock starting to rack her body with shivers, despite the fact that she was sure to have nightmares for the next month of that moment under the mill when she was sure she was going to die, Pauline was satisfied.

She was sorry for Dan's family, but she couldn't regret her actions. This was her place of peace. Not in a bucolic country village that only, perhaps, existed in city folk's imaginations. Not even in her scholarly accomplishments.

Rather, she found her strength and her sense of purpose in pursuing justice for the oppressed and in remaining faithful to the truth no matter how ugly. This was her way of lighting a candle against the dark.

At the end of the day, it was enough.

The End

Acknowledgements:

Many thanks to A. M. Offenwanger and Laura Rizzo, for reading this in its earlier stages and helping to make it what it is now; to Carl Ayers for editing and proofreading; to Kevin Bates for his encouragement and support and answering all my questions no matter how random; to Linda Casserly, the Canton Town and Village Historian, for her help in pointing me toward resources (and for maintaining the wonderful Facebook page with all its old photographs); and to all the people on Twitter and Facebook who said YES when I asked if anyone would read a story about a woman detective in northern New York in the 1930s.

www.ingramcontent.com/pod-product-compliance
Lightning Source LLC
Chambersburg PA
CBHW030559130626
46552CB00006B/2604